At first, Matt believed the black mass that occupied the corpse's skull was Edwin Locke's brain.

He thought that death had turned his brain that color. Then he saw that the mass pulsed like a heartbeat.

"Oh, my," Emma gasped.

The black mass leaped at Emma, evacuating the empty skull of the dead man with a sucking noise that echoed throughout the room. Emma screamed and raised her arms to protect her face as the creature flew toward her.

Matt was in motion at once, but Jesse Quinn was there before him. The American threw out an arm and swept Emma away as if the action were something she did every day. Her other hand had already drawn one of the .44 revolvers from her belt.

The creature flared in midair, its bulbous head splitting into the three-pronged claw that resembled a chicken's foot. The tentacles at its posterior end were no longer short and weak. Now they were thick and strong and stretched at least three feet long. The tentacles whipped forward toward Jessie's face, sliding around the bulbous mass and joining the three-toed claw in the blink of an eye. Matt had never seen anything move so quickly. . . .

HUNTER'S LEAGUE

A Conspiracy Revealed

The Mystery Unravels

And coming soon:

The Secret Explodes

HUNTER'S LEAGUE

THE MYSTERY UNRAVELS

MEL ODOM

SIMON PULSE
New York London Toronto Sydney

This book is a work of fiction. Any references to historical events, real people, or real locales are used fictitiously. Other names, characters, places, and incidents are the product of the author's imagination, and any resemblance to actual events or locales or persons, living or dead, is entirely coincidental.

SIMON PULSE
An imprint of Simon & Schuster Children's Publishing Division
1230 Avenue of the Americas, New York, NY 10020
Copyright © 2005 by Mel Odom
All rights reserved, including the right of reproduction in whole or in part in any form.
SIMON PULSE and colophon are registered trademarks of Simon & Schuster, Inc.
Designed by Sammy Yuen
The text of this book was set in Palatino.
Manufactured in the United States of America
First Simon Pulse edition July 2005
10 9 8 7 6 5 4 3 2 1

Library of Congress Control Number 2004115072
ISBN 0-689-86633-X

For Chandler and Jackson: the two-headed alien!

THE MYSTERY UNRAVELS

Chapter 1

London, England
1887

Dodging low-hanging branches, Matt Hunter rode the galloping horse through the night-steeped woods. The light rain that had come with the evening had long since drenched his clothing. He fervently hoped the shadows draped across Hackney Marsh didn't disguise a hole that he or the horse might see too late to avoid.

Hackney Marsh held wetlands and patches of forest that hadn't yet been cleared by builders or families laying up wood for winter. Much of the immediate area was uninhabitable, covered by standing water and islands of brush and weeds that refused to die.

Matt didn't know how many unmarked graves lay in the marshlands. In his seventeen years, he'd heard dozens of stories about thieves who had struck during the night. Some said the marshlands were haunted by restless spirits looking for retribution.

The trail wove between two thick stands of trees perched on knobby knees in pools of muck and dank water. Only a short distance ahead, a tree lay across the road. The white flesh of the tree gleamed in the moonlight, showing the marks of axes on its trunk and stump.

The horse's muscles bunched for a second, then the animal released and left the ground in a graceful arc that took it over the fallen tree. The treacherous ground gave way under the horse's hooves for a moment and the animal struggled to stay erect. Then it gathered itself and exploded forward again, staying with the trail.

Mist hung heavy in the air. Fogbanks coiled across the marsh. Small flickers of light played over the water.

Finally, when Matt was most beginning to doubt his chances of cutting cross-country to get ahead of his quarry, yellow coach lights glimmered in the distance, jerking between the boles of trees. The lights carved tunnels through the darkness and the rain.

The horse's breath came out in gray gusts. Matt felt sorry for the animal. He'd nearly pushed the horse to its death during the run from London.

"Stay with me," Matt said, patting the horse on the side of the neck. "Our race is nearly run."

The horse snorted and flicked its ears.

Matt reached to the back of the saddle, sliding free the British military rifle he'd outfitted himself with. Dressed in black as he was—boots, breeches, shirt, and long woolen coat—Matt knew the coach driver wouldn't see him till it was too late. He held the rifle in both hands and pulled the horse to a stop in the middle of Stratford Road.

Fear mixed with the anger that filled him. He didn't know what to expect. He'd never accosted a coach before, but he knew that drivers didn't take well to highwaymen.

And if the driver is directly in Creighdor's control, Matt told himself as he watched the coach lights come closer, *blood will spill tonight.*

The prospect chilled him, but he knew he wouldn't falter. He'd already slain men in his pursuit of his father's killer.

The coach approached. Creaks of the vehicle and the jingle of the harness mixed with the drumming of horses' hooves. Its lights came closer, then washed over him.

The driver, a large, burly man with long chin whiskers and a tall hat, spotted Matt. He leaned back in the seat for just an instant.

"Stop!" Matt ordered in the most authoritative voice he could muster. His command was all but lost in the sudden crack of thunder.

In response, the coachman lashed the reins across the rumps of the two-horse team. The nervous animals surged forward as a jagged streak of lightning blazed through the sky and turned everything stark blue-white for a moment. The sudden lightning seemed to freeze the raindrops in the air, but they kept falling. And the coach kept coming.

The team missed Matt by mere inches. After the coach whizzed past him, Matt urged his horse into quick pursuit.

He caught up with the vehicle before it had gone a hundred yards. Guiding his mount along the side of the road, he rapidly overtook the team. Ahead, the road crossed a small bridge that spanned a particularly nasty bit of the marshlands.

Thrusting the rifle back into the saddle scabbard, Matt matched pace with the horse team. He leaned forward, staying balanced over his own mount, and seized the closer horse's halter in a fist.

Without warning, fire blazed through his arm. He cried out but stubbornly held onto the horse's harness. Gazing over his shoulder, he saw the coach driver hauling back his whip for another strike.

The second blow was off the mark, though. The whip laid open the side of the horse's face, narrowly missing the poor creature's eye. Surprised by the sudden agony as well as another flash of lightning and a peal of thunder, the horse bolted to the right, aiming straight at the corner of the bridge.

Almost too late, the horse on the other side muscled its companion back toward the bridge.

Both horses shoved Matt's mount aside, but they failed to bring the coach back properly.

The vehicle's right front wheel missed the flat bridge entirely. Caught, the coach jerked to a stop, causing both horses to rear violently and nearly fall.

Matt wheeled his own horse around, bringing it to a stop on the other side of the short bridge. Leaning precariously, the coach gave up the losing battle against gravity and fell into the dank water of the marshland.

With a horrendous oath, the driver tumbled from the seat. He fell into the muck face-first.

Moving instantly, Matt grabbed the rifle from the scabbard again and swung down from his horse. He looped the reins around a nearby bush and walked toward the driver.

Lightning blazed again as the man raised himself from the muck and extended a hand in front of him. For a moment Matt didn't know he'd been shot. The lightning and thunder masked the muzzle flash and the detonation of gunpowder. He thought the burning pain in his right shoulder had been inflicted by the whip. He staggered, though, and that warned him.

The driver's second shot came only a second later, while he still lay in the marshland. The second bullet missed Matt's head by inches.

Pulling the rifle to his shoulder, aiming by instinct and training, Matt fired. The rifle kicked painfully into his wounded arm.

Sparks flared to brief life as the pistol leaped from the driver's hand and dropped somewhere in the muck.

Matt levered another round into the breech and kept walking toward the driver. Without hesitation he entered the dank water. He would not turn away from the man.

"My 'and!" the driver squalled in fear and pain. "You've gone an' ruined my 'and!"

The coach lay in the water behind the man. One of the lights was immersed, but the other burned steadily on the vehicle's side. The light was enough to show the man's mangled hand bleeding profusely. The round had taken off two or more fingers.

The grisly sight nearly unnerved Matt. He'd seen worse wounds, but he'd never gotten used to them. Hitting the man's hand and knocking the pistol away had been luck. He'd aimed at the man's arm, intending to disable him. Still, all he had to do was remember his father's horrible death to tighten his resolve.

"If you have any more surprises," Matt threatened as he continued walking, "another pistol—or even a knife—I give you my word that I'll put a bullet between your eyes and leave you for the swamp rats."

"Don't!" the man pleaded. He came to his knees, water up to his waist, and held his injured hand to his chest. "Don't kill me! I ain't done nothin' to deserve killin' over!"

Matt kept the rifle pointed at the center of the driver's chest. "Lucius Creighdor," Matt said in a cold voice.

The man looked at Matt and did his best to appear confused. "I don' know what you're talkin' about. 'Onest, I don't."

"You're transporting a package for Creighdor," Matt said. Creighdor was constantly shipping things into and out of London.

"I'm 'aulin' cargo," the man agreed. "Don't know no one named Creighdor." The man's eyelids fluttered.

"You're lying," Matt said. "You were seen taking a package from one of his people."

The man hiccuped his fear. He tried to speak twice and couldn't.

Matt waited. Silence was often more threatening.

Shaking his head, his voice breaking, the driver spoke in a hoarse voice. "Creighdor will *kill* me!"

"What do you think *I* will do?"

The man shook his head and mewled. Knowing he was the cause of the man's fear sickened Matt.

"I want the package," Matt said. Cold from the marsh water ate through his knee-high riding boots and penetrated his bones. "I don't want to hurt you."

"You ruined my 'and," the man accused. "I ain't never gonna be the same."

For an instant, uncertainty brushed Matt, as

chill and insistent as the water and the fog surrounding them. What right did he have to pursue his mission of vengeance as far as he had?

Then he hardened his heart. His father had fought the battle for seven long years, since Creighdor or Scanlon or both had murdered Matt's mother. If anyone had a right, he did.

"The package," Matt repeated.

After only a brief hesitation, the driver said, "It's up under the seat, it is. I've got an 'idey-'ole there. For important stuff."

And for contraband, Matt told himself. Keeping the rifle pointed at the man, he crossed to the overturned coach and reached up under the driver's seat to find the hidden area. He took a small knife from his boot top and cut the leather hinges. The front fell open. A small box was nestled inside.

Mesmerized, knowing that he was about to put his hands on another of Creighdor's secrets, Matt reached in for the package. Movement at the edge of his vision warned him that the driver was up to something.

Snapping his head around, Matt watched as the driver shook a small revolver from inside his left sleeve. He brought the weapon level with unbelievable speed. A madman's smile twisted his lower face.

Chapter 2

Matt tried to bring his rifle to bear, but there wasn't enough time. The man's revolver spat flame and a bullet dug wooden splinters from the coach next to Matt's ear.

Then the driver's head snapped back as a neat round hole formed in the center of his forehead. He went stiff-legged and fell backward into the water.

Horses' hooves slapped the wet ground to Matt's right, coming back along the road from Hackney and London. He stayed close to the coach and peered down the road. It was possible that Creighdor had sent men to kill him and the driver. The driver could have been a casualty of his own mates.

Two figures on horseback appeared under a blaze of lightning. As they neared the overturned coach, the warm flames of the surviving lantern brought them out of the darkness a little more.

"Matt!" a voice called.

"Paul?" Matt relaxed, but only a little, as he recognized his friend's voice. Paul Chadwick-Standish was a friend since childhood, one of only two who had stayed true after Lady Brockton's mysterious murder and Lord Brockton's apparent madness had settled in.

Even in wet traveling clothes, Paul was elegant. He was lean as a rapier and had blazing red hair that looked burnished in the lantern light. He carried a rifle in his hand.

"It's me," Paul said. He gazed at the dead man, obviously not happy with what he saw.

"An' me," another male voice called.

Gabriel was another friend, but only of the past few years, when Matt's loneliness had driven him to despair and he'd sought solace in London's streets at night. Gabriel was also an accomplished thief with a horde of young homeless and near-to-homeless boys who worked with him. He had a thick shock of shoulder-length black hair he kept pulled back, and depthless black eyes. He was shorter than Paul, being only a few inches over five feet, but looked more wiry.

"Are you all right?" Paul asked as he pulled his horse to a stop on the bridge.

"Yes. Was it you who made that shot?" Matt noticed that Gabriel wasn't carrying a rifle, and the distance had surely been too far for a pistol.

"Yes." Paul glanced at the dead man floating in the dark water and looked pained.

"'E very nearly 'ad you," Gabriel announced. "'E 'ad you dead in 'is sights, 'e did. Why, if'n Paul 'adn't made such a fine shot, like as not you wouldn't be 'ere, mate."

Matt waded through the water to reclaim his horse. He pulled himself into the saddle just as Gabriel tossed his reins to Paul and dismounted.

"I wasn't aware that you knew how to ride, Gabriel," Matt said.

Gabriel frowned as he walked through the marsh water. "Not something I often lay claim to, an' not somethin' I much enjoy. I prefer me own two feet to get me around. Still, I knew I wasn't gonna be able to keep up with you on me own." He knelt, keeping his body just out of the water, and began going through the dead man's pockets.

"You're robbing him?" Paul asked, incredulously.

"Why not?" Gabriel responded. "It ain't like we're rushed at this point, is it?" He dropped the dead man's coins into his pockets. "An' I promise, you ain't gonna get much off of ol' Fat Willie. 'E wasn't one to be 'angin' on to wealth." A watch disappeared into Gabriel's pocket. "Always spendin' it, 'e was."

"You knew him?" Paul asked.

"I did," Gabriel admitted. "Wasn't proud of it, an' 'e weren't no friend of mine. Fat Willie, 'e was a bad 'un." He glanced at Paul. "You ain't gotta feel bad about doin' for 'im. Fat Willie, 'e only 'ad one claim to fame." He stood. "'E killed 'is wife, 'e did. Only the peelers couldn't prove it."

"Why couldn't the police prove it?" Paul asked.

Gabriel looked up and grinned. "'Cause Fat Willie ate 'er."

Paul grimaced. "That made him famous? The fact that he got away with murdering his poor wife?"

"Oh, 'is wife was no saint. She'd murdered people a time or two. It's just that she was so, so bloomin' *fat*." Gabriel held his arms out to demonstrate enormous girth. "'E ate *all* of 'er. That's what made 'im famous."

"That's a positively horrid story," Paul commented.

"An' all of it true." Gabriel held up a hand. "My 'and to God. That's why you shouldn't feel bad about pottin' 'im."

"I won't," Paul promised earnestly.

Matt rode his horse over to the coach team, slipping off their harnesses so they could run free.

"You're injured," Paul said, riding over to him. "I saw blood." He caught the bridle of Matt's horse and turned the animal around so the lantern light fell across Matt's wounded arm. Blood gleamed in threads that ran down Matt's hand, only slightly crimson in the rain and the darkness.

"I'll live," Matt replied. He pulled out the

package he'd gotten from the coach's hiding place. "I've got Creighdor's delivery."

Plain brown paper covered the square object. He pulled at the paper but found that the covering, even though wet, didn't easily yield its secrets.

"Don't open it here," Paul said. "It could be booby-trapped."

"I hadn't considered that." Reluctantly Matt put the package under his woolen coat. He glanced at the dead man floating facedown in the water. "Seems like a lot of trouble to have gone to."

"Creighdor doesn't want his secrets known. A booby trap could be designed to destroy the contents rather than the person who intercepted it. Whatever secrets the package holds, it can keep them till we're back in London."

By the time they reached the city and stabled the horses with a hostler Gabriel knew, Matt was drenched, chilled to the bone with the cold weather and the fever that had gripped him during the ride. He was also nervous. He'd never been shot before and he didn't know how badly he was hurt. The wounded shoulder throbbed constantly.

Although it was now almost one o'clock in the morning, London wasn't yet abed. Lantern lights blazed in several businesses and apartments. Dark gray smudges of smoke from the factory chimneys stood out against the black clouds that filled the sky and blotted out the stars.

They took a hansom cab to the East End. From there Gabriel guided them through a twisted maze of alleyways between businesses and flats. They arrived finally at a basement space that had once housed a leather shop. Matt knew that only from the splintered and faded wooden sign hanging beside the door. During the past few days Gabriel had kept them on the move throughout London's seamier neighborhoods, never using the same spot twice. Creighdor's men diligently searched for them and the prize they held.

Gabriel worked his skills with his lock picks and let them inside the shop.

"If you get caught with those lock picks," Paul pointed out, "it'll be a short trip to Newgate Prison for you. And likely a sudden drop at the end of a rope."

In the darkness inside the shop, Gabriel grinned. He doffed his hat and shook the rain from it. "An' which would you 'ave me more worried about? Bobbies I been gettin' away from all me life? Or the likes of Creighdor an' 'is lackeys?"

"If you're caught with us," Paul said, "we could get locked up as well."

"Trust me," Gabriel said, "no one will ever find 'em. Stay 'ere. I'll fetch a light for us."

Matt stood and felt the rain dripping around him. The room had a musty smell that spoke of months of being closed up. No one had been there in a long time. Gabriel's knowledge of what places were available continually amazed him.

The thief made his way through the darkness as surely as a bat. Metal clanked and a lucifer fired. He touched the match to a candlewick, catching it aflame, then dropping the glass back into place. Dim orange light belled out from the candle but didn't quite touch the stained walls.

Paul glanced around the shop's empty shelves and looked clearly unhappy. Pieces of cast-off leather littered the dirty floor. "This filth is hardly the place to bring Matt when he's wounded."

Gabriel took no offense. "It's the best we got. Beggars can't be choosers." He pulled out a chair and tapped it. "Sit 'ere, Matt. Let's 'ave a look at your arm."

Feeling weak and a little sick, the fever drumming between his temples, Matt sat. Gabriel helped him undress, stripping him to the waist.

"Lucky," Gabriel commented, poking at his shoulder. "The ball went clean through."

Flinching from the pain, Matt said, "Luck would have meant I'd not been hit at all."

"Well now, there's different degrees of luck, ain't there?"

"The wound will have to be cleaned," Paul

said. "There could be all manner of infectious material inside." He fingered the torn edges of Matt's shirt. "Some of the cloth from his shirt or his coat could be in there. That could be enough to cause corruption to set in."

Matt studied the hole in his shoulder. The exit wound was nearly twice the size of the entry wound. The hole was bruised and black. Surely nothing remained inside. But the thought was a sobering one. A number of sailors and dock-workers had missing limbs due to gangrenous infections from wounds poorly tended.

"I could patch 'im up right enough," Gabriel stated, "but I ain't no proper doctor, I ain't. Don't feel comfortable going in after whatever might be in there. I could 'urt 'im just as much as I could 'elp 'im." Worry creased his narrow face.

"I can't do it," Paul said. "He needs a physician."

"Going to a physician is out of the question," Matt said. "There would be too many questions, and we don't know how many resources Creighdor has."

"We'll need Mr. Chaudhary's assistance in this." Paul looked at Gabriel. Narada Chaudhary was a Hindu antiquities dealer who had crossed paths with Creighdor in the past and was now part of Matt's undeclared army striving to bring the man down. "Can you send one of your lads around to fetch him?"

Gabriel nodded and stepped outside. "I'll be

back soon as I can." He closed the door afterward.

Ignoring the jabbing pain in his shoulder and the fiery ache in his head, Matt put the package on the nearby workbench. He slipped the knife from his boot top and slid the blade under the brown paper, angling it to slice the twine wrapped round the package. Before he knew it, he was holding his breath.

Behind the glass, the candle flame flickered.

Surprisingly, Matt's hands remained steady. He cut through the twine and teased the paper open with the knife blade. A patch of lacquered cherrywood showed through.

When the paper was peeled away, the object stood revealed. The box was a perfect cube, perhaps five inches across in all three directions, and showed signs of age. Old scars marred the red finish.

Beeswax held a Z-shaped brass bar on one face. A slot in another face looked rather like a keyhole.

Paul stepped closer, still wary of the box. His voice was thick with disgust. "Do you know what it is?"

"No."

"It's a child's jack-in-the-box."

Matt tapped the box with the knife blade. "Perhaps." But he knew it could be something much worse. He turned the box over and used the blade to pry at the lid. The wood splintered.

Knowing he was only going to break the box, he prized the key from the beeswax, then fitted it into the keyhole. He turned the lever, listening to gears ratcheting inside as the spring inside grew tighter and tighter.

Without warning the top opened and a garish figure sprang out. Even though he'd been prepared for the explosion of movement, Matt nearly dropped the thing.

Paul cursed.

It was a clown. At least, the description fit the nominal requirements for being a clown. It had a jester's cap, bushy hair, and a painted face.

But instead of a smile or a sad look, the clown bore a look of total malice. The white face powder was the jaundiced color of old bone. Inverted black triangles covered the eyes and made the raptor's beak of a nose stand out even more prominently. The rouged lips drew back in a wolfish snarl, baring pointed shark's teeth that didn't quite meet. In both hands the clown gripped wicked knives that bounced and stabbed the air.

Then a voice that sounded at once cultured and totally mad came out of the box. "Stay away, Matthew Hunter! Stay away or you shall surely die!"

Chapter 3

Creighdor's mockin' us, 'e is. Tryin' to show us 'ow much smarter 'e is than we are."

Matt couldn't disagree with Gabriel's assessment of the night's events. He stared at the wicked jack-in-the-box on the table. The figure leaned over, looking like a puppet with most of its strings cut.

"Creighdor is warning you," Narada Chaudhary said in his quiet voice. He sat on a stool at Matt's side while tending to the gunshot wound in Matt's shoulder.

In his early fifties, Chaudhary stood a little over five and a half feet tall. His dark complexion and graying black hair and beard spoke of his origins in India. He had left his native country some years ago and brought his family to London to operate a small import/export shop specializing in antiquities. He wore shopkeeper's clothing, complete with a leather apron stained with Matt's blood.

"Warning us?" Paul challenged. "That driver would have killed Matt. He tried. And he very nearly succeeded."

"I do not think that was Creighdor's intent," Chaudhary said. "He planned for you to find the package. If the driver had killed Matt, I should think Creighdor would have been very vexed."

"Why?" Paul demanded. "Given the circumstances, I would be more inclined to believe that Creighdor would want Matt dead."

"Creighdor doesn't yet have Lord Brockton's missing book."

A brief image of the book about Creighdor that his father had shown him—painstakingly compiled by Lord Brockton over the years—flashed through Matt's mind. He had barely looked at the book, barely heard some of the stories his father had to tell, before one of the mysterious animated gargoyles under the control of Creighdor and his minions arrived and killed Roger Hunter.

Sometimes, when Matt was all alone and the nervous energy that filled him quieted, he could almost remember the drawings and pictures that had been in that book. Unfortunately, his memories were all of his father's portraits of his mother. That book had been lost in the fire that had consumed the apartment building where Roger Hunter had been murdered.

"We don't know if there is another book," Matt said. But the strange key his father had left for him, now hanging around his neck, reminded him that *something* was hidden. And it had let him know that Lord Brockton had been more attentive to secrets than Matt had believed. His father had always told him that the only way two men could keep a secret was if one of them was dead.

After finding out about the first book, Gabriel had deduced that Lord Brockton had kept a second book, as so many businessmen did. That had yet to be proven, though.

And even if it does exist, Matt thought tiredly, *it's probably lost forever.*

"Creighdor came to you looking for the book in Mayfair," Chaudhary reminded.

That encounter would have cost Paul's life if Creighdor had had his way. Paul's hand leaped to his neck, absently stroking the small pink scar there.

"Creighdor could be wrong as well." But Matt remembered how certain Creighdor had been that the book existed. The man might not have looked fearful about the possibility, but he had been concerned enough to send men after Paul and Matt.

"Yes." Chaudhary reached into the small medical kit he'd brought with him. "If Creighdor chooses to believe the book does not exist, I think things will go very differently for all of us. You are still new to this fight against Creighdor. You have much to learn about his predatory nature."

Matt silently accepted that. Narada Chaudhary had encountered Lucius Creighdor back in his country years ago. That seemed impossible given Creighdor's apparent youthful appearance, that of a man in his mid-twenties, but Chaudhary insisted Creighdor was the man who had taken his brother's life more than a dozen years ago. An investigation into Egyptian imports had brought Roger Hunter to Chaudhary's shop months ago. Lord Brockton had brought Creighdor's presence to Chaudhary's attention, and Chaudhary had given Lord Brockton information about his foe.

Following up on the information he'd ferreted out after his father's death, Matt had tracked his father's trail back to the mysterious mummy that Creighdor had been after.

In the end, after discovering what Creighdor had done, Matt and his friends had stolen aboard a ketch to examine the mummy. While aboard *Saucy Lass*, Matt had seen the mummy's eyes glow and project moving pictures of ancient Egypt. The moving pictures beamed from the mummy's head were among a growing list of Creighdor's secrets that Matt had yet to fathom.

Desperate to learn the mummy's secrets and knowing it was of value to his father's killer, Matt had used a cooper's saw to amputate the head and take it with him during their escape from the ship.

Over the past few days Matt had learned that Creighdor's people were somehow able to track the head. Groups of men roved London in search of it. As a result, Gabriel had kept some of his boys moving the head through the city, stopping now and again for short times to allow Chaudhary chances to uncover the secrets it held.

"Have you had any luck with the mummy's head?" Paul asked.

"No." Chaudhary reached into his kit and took out a curved needle. "That head and the box it contains are very frustrating. I fear it is beyond my limited understanding."

Matt noted how tired the man looked. Meeting with Gabriel's boys in the middle of the night didn't leave much time for Chaudhary's family or running his antique business.

Paul tapped his walking stick against the floor. It was a nervous habit he had. He took his pocketwatch from his vest and checked the time.

"Matt," Paul began. "I think we should consider bringing Emma into—"

"No," Matt said.

Paul frowned and put his watch away. "Emma has a good grasp of science." He stopped. "I mean no disrespect, Mr. Chaudhary."

"No offense taken," Chaudhary responded. "A man must know his limitations. I recognized mine a long time ago. I am a keeper of all things old. If you want to know legends or mythologies,

I can help you. But this?" He shook his head. "I struggle with science."

Paul tried again. "Matt, Emma would be—"

"In danger," Matt interrupted. "I'll not allow that. It's bad enough that I've gotten you and Gabriel involved in this."

"Oh, I don't mind so much," Gabriel said laconically. He dusted his fingernails across his shirt. "So far, it ain't been without a spot of fun. An' the chance at nickin' some cash or other valuables from a man like Creighdor who don't truly deserve all that 'e's got? I'm in for somethin' like that any time."

"If what your father suspected is true, and I'm beginning to believe that it is after seeing how deeply entrenched Creighdor is in the finances of London, we would have crossed swords sooner or later," Paul said. "You at least provided me a running start into the fray."

Matt was silently grateful to have the friends he had. Sometimes he didn't feel like he deserved them, especially in light of the way he'd turned away from his own father and believed Roger Hunter had gone mad with grief over his dead wife. During the last seven years, Matt had committed himself to nothing but a day-to-day existence with no thoughts to a future.

"We need to know the head's secret," Paul repeated.

Matt said nothing, biting back a cry of pain as Chaudhary poked at his wounded shoulder.

"Or we need to get rid of the 'ead," Gabriel added.

"We're not getting rid of the head," Matt said in a tight voice. "Not till I'm certain we're done with it. For now, that head is all we have to go on."

"Creighdor's blokes are gettin' better about searchin' it out," Gabriel said.

Matt wasn't surprised. They had seen three of Creighdor's men carrying small devices on two different occasions when they'd nearly found the head. The devices looked similar to the boxes they used to control the gargoyles.

"My lads are 'avin' to jump it about sometimes twice a night now," Gabriel went on. "Them men searchin' for it, they're figurin' out our strategies. I only got so many 'idin' places I can put it. Sooner or later, they'll catch up to us."

Matt felt the pressure to do something building inside him. He mastered the pain of Chaudhary's ministrations, trying to push it away from him. The opiate drink Chaudhary had given him to dull the pain of the cleansing made his head swim.

"I understand," Matt said.

"That's all good an' well," Gabriel said, "but I don't want a single one of them boys what I'm lookin' out for 'urt."

The young thief looked after a number of younger boys who couldn't take care of themselves out on the street. Matt had never fully realized the responsibility Gabriel carried until the last few days. He'd always thought Gabriel was simply well known to the street urchins.

"Neither do I."

"It comes down to it, Matt," Gabriel promised, "why I'll see that 'ead sunk to the bottom of the Thames with that ship if I 'ave to."

During the escape from the ship, *Saucy Lass* had caught fire. The crew had shoved her out into the river and she'd burned to the waterline.

"Another few days," Matt said. "Let's just give it another few days."

"How are you feeling?" Chaudhary asked. "Do you need more opiate?"

"I'm fine," Matt insisted. "My head is fair to floating off my shoulders as it is."

"The wound is clean," Chaudhary said, "but I need to suture it."

"Do it," Matt said. He closed his eyes as he felt the needle bite into his shoulder.

The next four days passed in relative peace. Matt's arm stayed sore for the first two days, but he quickly regained the use of it. Gabriel's spies kept watch over Creighdor's people but ultimately learned nothing. The men searching for the mummy head closed the net they had over the city. Twice over the intervening nights, Matt had seen gargoyles overhead. He kept watch on the morning of the fifth day while riding in Paul's rented coach.

"Are you awake?"

Drawn from his reverie, and perhaps a moment or two of sleep, Matt glanced across the coach at Paul.

As usual when doing business, Paul dressed elegantly in a coat and tails. He'd even purchased a new hat. He repeated his question, a little louder and more insistent this time.

"I'm awake," Matt said.

Paul smiled. "Good."

The driver turned off Fleet Street and headed south toward the river. The high peaks of Blackfriars Bridge poked above the close-set buildings containing living quarters and businesses. People filled the street, hurrying to and fro in their daily pursuits, causing the coachman to drive more carefully.

"I didn't know we had business in Southwark," Matt said.

Paul answered without ceasing his study of the notes in his journal. "We don't. We've business on this side of the river."

"What business?"

"We're having a meeting with Mr. Jonathan Pender."

Matt raised his eyebrows.

"You don't remember, do you?"

"No."

Paul sighed. "Your mind is a sieve, it truly is."

Matt didn't argue although he knew that wasn't true. His attention was focused solely on Creighdor these days.

"We're here to see Mr. Pender about a business proposition," Paul explained. "He makes glassware of all kinds, from dishes to windows to stained glass lamps. His products have started selling faster abroad, and he's increased the productivity of his manufacturing plant. As a result, he's in need of ships to transport some of his wares to the overseas markets he's developed. You have trading ships in need of cargo. I thought it expedient to put the two needs together."

After his father's death, Matt had inherited his father's title, estates, and businesses.

The family barrister had advised Matt to sell the businesses and live off the proceeds. Matt hadn't been able to do that. Losing the rest of his father's businesses would have meant accepting a major defeat at Creighdor's hands. Instead he had asked Paul to manage the businesses and teach him what he needed to know. Paul managed his own business interests with cunning aplomb, always teaching himself new things.

Running businesses, though, held no allure for Matt. It wasn't until Paul had pointed out the possibility of using those assets in his war against Creighdor that Matt had been able to rouse any interest. He wasn't rich by any means, but he was comfortable.

The driver guided the horse down a narrow side street. Matt felt claustrophobic under the press of the close-set buildings. He scanned the ledges for gargoyles and found four of them.

"I see them," Paul said. "But so far none has moved."

The driver halted a short time later and rushed around to the side of the cab. Paul went out through the open door but came to a stop on the step.

"There is a problem," Paul said in a quiet voice. He pointed with his chin at a sleek black brougham coach sitting in front of a large building that bore the sign PENDER GLASSWORKS.

"What?" Matt asked.

"That coach belongs to Lucius Creighdor," Paul answered.

Chapter 4

What business would Creighdor have here?" Matt followed Paul through the elegant entrance of Pender Glassworks. The door was trimmed in stained glass that caught the morning sun.

Inside, the room was huge, filled with windows and other glassware. Smartly dressed salesmen showed potential buyers around.

"Any business Creighdor would have here wouldn't be to our best interests, you can be sure of that." Paul flagged down one of the clerks, then quickly explained that they were there to see Mr. Jonathan Pender. He handed the clerk his card.

The clerk returned in short order and said Pender would see them down in his private offices. The clerk led the way.

Once through the main showroom and three smaller showrooms done up to look like a dining room, a banquet hall, and a cottage, the clerk led them to the basement. The steep stairs turned in on themselves four times and plunged down into darkness, causing Matt to go on alert even more.

The basement was carved deep into the ground. A long tunnel dimly lit by oil lanterns took them to the glassworks factory. Cinders crunched underfoot and soot covered the cavern walls, which showed old bite marks from picks and shovels.

They rounded a corner and a warm golden glow filled the tunnel. Only a short distance later, Matt found himself standing in the glass foundry.

Two dozen men worked at the huge furnace that took up one side of the cavernous underground room. Coal burned bright orange in the bed of the furnace. Boys operated the bellows pump to keep air blowing across the coals. The heat that filled the room pressed against Matt and covered him with perspiration in short order. He couldn't imagine working in such a place day after day.

Jonathan Pender's office was in the back on the wall opposite the giant furnace. The door was plain and unadorned, covered with dozens of old burn marks.

The clerk rapped on the door, knocking hard to be heard over the noisy bellows and the whoosh and crackle of the furnace flames.

"Enter," a man's deep voice called from within.

The clerk opened the door and stepped through, ushering Paul and Matt in after him. "Mr. Pender, I'd like to present Mr. Paul Chadwick-Standish and Lord Brockton. Gentlemen, Mr. Jonathan Pender, esteemed owner of Pender Glassworks."

Matt still felt uncomfortable being addressed by his family hereditary title.

On the other side of the small room, Jonathan Pender sat behind a large oak desk. He was a stout man of medium height, shoulders broadened from years of hard work and a belly big with the success he'd enjoyed. His fair hair was thick but going gray at the temples and down the muttonchop whiskers he favored. He wore a simple white shirt, the sleeves held up by garters, and a tie.

"Ah." Pender stood and smiled. "Mr. Chadwick-Standish, so good to see you again. And Lord Brockton, it is an honor to meet you, sir. Please." He gestured to the four overstuffed chairs in front of the desk. "Sit."

Paul and Matt sat.

"I hope we haven't taken you away from important business, Mr. Pender." Paul casually pulled off his gloves finger by finger. He maintained an air of the theatrical when he wished.

"Of course not, Mr. Chadwick-Standish, of course not." Pender waved the suggestion away.

"We had this meeting scheduled. I appreciate your promptness."

"Time is money, Mr. Pender."

"Yes, it is." Pender's eyes surveyed Matt. "Do you know much about glassware, Lord Brockton?"

"Unfortunately, less than I should," Matt replied. "I only know that Mr. Chadwick-Standish tells me you are the very best in all of London."

A proud smile curved Pender's full lips. "As crass as it may be, I shall lay claim to that generous accolade." He toasted them with his glass. He reached into his desk drawer and took out a small blue bottle of pills. He rolled two pink tablets onto his palm, popped them into his mouth, and swallowed. A look of distaste soured his features. "Doctor's prescription, I'm afraid. I've been experiencing chronic earaches. I'm almost convinced the cure is worse than the ailment."

"I took the liberty of having our barrister draw up the papers." Paul reached inside his coat and took out a thick sheaf of papers, placing them on the desk.

Pender made no move to take the documents. He frowned uncomfortably, like a man who'd eaten something that hadn't agreed with him. "I appreciate the effort, Mr. Chadwick-Standish. However, I find that I cannot accept the agreement today."

"I assure you, Mr. Pender," Paul said conversationally, "that the terms of the agreement are to the letter. Exactly as we worked them out."

"I have no doubt that they are," Pender agreed.

"Then why don't you accept the offer?" Matt demanded. His voice carried more of an edge to it than he'd wanted. But he was tired and irritable, and he wasn't ready to accept the setback. He couldn't believe Paul was taking everything so calmly.

Pender hesitated. "I've been given a better offer."

"A better offer?" Matt couldn't believe it. "You made a gentleman's agreement with Paul. A gentleman's word should be worth something."

Pender erupted from his chair. His beefy face went red at once. "How dare you, you . . . you ignorant whelp! You don't know one iota about business! If it were not for Mr. Chadwick-Standish's involvement, you'd already be a penniless pauper."

The accusation made Matt's face burn with embarrassment: He knew it was true.

"Mr. Pender," Paul began.

"Perhaps I don't know much about business affairs, but I know I've got sailors that need jobs," Matt roared back. "I know your agreement promised them jobs."

Pender waved a hand dismissively. "Your

problems are none of my affair. And your problems are part of the reason I have changed my mind about entering into an agreement with you."

"My problems," Matt said, leaning over the desk, "are going to be solved. I am going to solve them with Paul's help."

"I had been promised that the Hunter family problems had ended with the death of your father," Pender said. "Instead I find you carrying on in much the same manner as he did."

"What are you talking about?"

Pender reached into his desk and pulled out a stack of newspapers. "I'm talking about the fight that you had with a Scotland Yard inspector."

The Scotland Yard inspector had been George Donovan. Donovan had arrived at Paul's parents' house to collect Matt after his father's death. At the site where the building had blown up after the gargoyle had killed Roger Hunter, Donovan's insufferable accusations had become too much. Matt had reacted violently and some of the London newspaper reporters had been on hand.

The newspaper printed pictures of Matt and his father. Some of the headlines screamed, MAD LORD RESPONSIBLE FOR DESTRUCTION OF SELF AND PROPERTY and YOUNG LORD BROCKTON INHERITS FAMILY TITLE AND HEREDITARY INSANITY.

"Those are lies," Matt said in a cold voice. "My father did not take his own life. He was murdered."

"I am not here for a debate, Lord Brockton," Pender said. "I was unaware of these stories. I work very hard at my business. It feeds not only my family, but several others besides." He rapped a fist against the stack of papers.

"You can't afford to let your warehouses fill up with product that you can't ship," Paul said.

Pender didn't answer.

"You have signed with someone else," Paul said.

Pender remained silent.

"Might I inquire who you signed an agreement with?" Paul asked.

"I'd rather not say," Pender replied.

"Oh, do tell them," an unctuous voice said.

Matt recognized Lucius Creighdor's voice immediately. Turning, he spotted Creighdor standing at the door. Neither he nor Paul had heard the door open.

Lucius Creighdor stood a couple inches taller than Matt, topping six feet. He was slim and elegant, but had the sallow complexion of a man who did not often greet the day. His dark hair was drawn back in a queue and his bangs hung down slightly into his dark eyes. He wore a mustache and neatly cut goatee. He leaned on an ornate walking stick covered with strange markings.

Matt kept his gaze on Creighdor, the man responsible for the death of both of his parents. The Webley was tight in Matt's hand. For a moment he thought of pulling the pistol free and putting a bullet between the man's eyes.

"Would that be the wisest course of action, boy?" Creighdor taunted.

Matt started to pull the pistol from his coat pocket. Then Paul was there, walking into Matt and trapping his arm.

"Perhaps, Mr. Chadwick-Standish," Creighdor said, "it would be best if you escorted young Lord Brockton from these premises."

"No," Paul whispered again, never taking his eyes from Matt's. "Not here. Not now. Trust me, Matt, our time will come. But this is not it. Remember what we talked about."

Since the violent confrontation with Inspector Donovan, Paul had pointed out that attacking Creighdor in public could work against Matt. If Matt were found guilty and locked away, Creighdor could buy the family estates from the tax collectors for a pittance. If Lord Brockton's second book did exist, and if it was on the family estates, it could be lost forever.

Giving in to his friend's calm and good sense, Matt allowed himself to be led away. He felt Creighdor's eyes boring into his back, and he could feel the weight of the man's smug smile.

Chapter 5

Once more in the furnace room, Matt broke Paul's grip on his arm. He couldn't stand being constrained any longer. Paul immediately took up a position to intercept Matt if he headed back toward the office.

"No," Matt said bitterly. "I'm done here. Creighdor has won."

"Creighdor hasn't won," Paul said, not stepping away. "This was just a skirmish. A brief battle. Nothing more."

"We needed Pender's cargoes."

"We did." Paul shrugged and nodded. "That's why we were here. But there are other avenues. Trust me. I have found them. I will work this out."

For the first time, Matt saw how tired his friend was. Although Paul hadn't been prowling the streets as Gabriel and Matt had, he'd kept his energies focused on other fronts of their struggles. Matt felt guilty.

He spun away, struggling to win over the emotions warring within him. Paul was trying to take care of him, and Matt had placed his friend in jeopardy. At the moment, combined with having to back down from Creighdor, it was almost too much.

A woman's sharp voice drew Matt's attention. He hadn't expected to hear a woman in the foundry. Looking around, he spotted her at once. She looked totally out of place.

Her skin was dark, marking her as a foreigner, and her hair was black as coal, even possessing some of the same blue highlights as the mineral. She looked lean and fit, her curves more defined in the bright blue dress she wore instead of the bustles that British women favored. Embroidery gleamed on the shoulders and hem. Her hair hung loose and free. Matching blue gloves covered her hands. It was obvious that she didn't work there. Matt guessed that she was visiting, perhaps picking out dishes.

She regarded Matt with interest. A collection of young workers gathered around her. One of them said something. Without taking her eyes from Matt, she said something back to the young man. He pressed his luck and stepped in closer. Quick as a striking snake, the young woman turned and punched the worker in the face so hard that he dropped to the ground and lay unmoving.

At first the other men were shocked, then

anger set in. Some of them called the woman vile names. She stood her ground with an amused smile, then unleashed a verbal barrage of her own that held only a smattering of English just as vitriolic as the words the men had used. Some of them were Spanish. Matt recognized them from the Spanish and Portuguese sailors working the docks on the Thames. None of them belonged in the mouth of a young woman.

Before he realized what he was doing, Matt crossed the distance and put himself between the woman and the workers.

"That will be enough of that," Matt said, addressing the men. His suit made him stand out from the crowd, cowing them instantly.

One of the burly men spat on the cinder-covered floor. "That woman's got no business down 'ere round workin' men. These men, they ain't proper gentlemen, an' she's stokin' 'em up."

"An' she's no lady," another said. "Sure, an' she's got a fine dress, she does. But she's impure. Just somebody's little rented bird showin' off her wares."

The young woman suddenly loosed another volley of what had to be curses and stepped around Matt. The man seized a pair of red-hot tongs from the nearby table, holding them up in menacing triumph.

A revolver appeared in the young woman's hand and she swept the weapon up, pointing directly at the offensive speaker. Her thumb pulled the hammer back as if she'd been performing the maneuver for years.

"Back in Texas where I come from," the woman said in an icy voice that held a strange accent Matt had never before heard, "a man would get horsewhipped for darin' to talk to a woman like that."

Matt was stunned. He'd never seen anyone produce a pistol so fast. The accent was American, but it was something more as well.

"Open that big yap of yours again," she threatened, "an' I'll put a bullet in it."

Despite the dress and the gloves, Matt felt the woman would do exactly what she said she'd do. The glassworkers must have believed her as well. They moved back in a group. None of them spoke.

"Perhaps," Paul suggested in a quiet voice, standing on the other side of the young woman, "we could take leave of this situation without killing anyone."

The woman didn't look away from the group of men. She kept her pistol leveled. "Who invited you to the party, fancy-pants?"

Paul was taken aback. "Excuse me?"

"You got something wrong with your ears?" the woman demanded. "I didn't stutter. You come around here pokin' your nose in other folks' business, you're liable to get it lopped off."

"Miss," Paul tried again, "would you allow my friend and me the honor of escorting you from these premises?"

"Why?" A condescending smile twisted the young woman's lips. "Are they making improper suggestions to you, too?"

Paul colored briefly and tried desperately to regain his aplomb. "No. I just thought—"

"It's not a problem, boys," she said. "I can get you out of here if you want."

"That's not what I was suggesting," Paul said. "I thought that we might get *you*—"

"Anybody ever tell you that you talk too much?" the young woman asked. She grabbed the front of Paul's jacket and pulled him into motion. "Just follow me an' stick close. Cowards usually strike the instant you turn your back." She added something in the foreign language.

In disbelief, Matt followed the woman. He really felt the men wouldn't pursue their harassment of her any further. Together the three of them made their way back through the tunnel, up the stairs, and through the showcase areas to the street. They stopped in front of Pender Glassworks in the full glare of the morning sun.

"Well now," the young woman said, grinning as she tucked her pistol back inside her handbag, "that was fun."

"Fun? That was your idea of *fun*?" Paul looked apoplectic.

"Sure," she replied, totally calm. "Gets your blood up. Makes you glad to be alive."

Matt looked at her, knowing at once that he'd never met anyone like her.

"Those men would have killed you," Paul said.

"No," she corrected. "They were only struttin'."

"'Strutting'?" Matt asked.

"Yes." She hooked her thumbs under her armpits and flapped her elbows. "Like a banty rooster. All prideful an' all, but you know a banty rooster ain't gonna stick around when the water gets hot."

Matt just stared at her.

The woman put her arms down and gave him a reproachful glance. "Surely even a city boy like you has seen a rooster. You know, a male chicken?"

"I've seen chickens," Matt replied. "And I'm no boy."

The young woman's lips twitched into a small smile. Up close, disconcertingly close for Matt though she gave no indication of feeling that way herself, he discovered that she was only a couple of inches shorter than his own five feet ten. She smelled like flowers.

"Well, good for you," she said.

Matt felt his anger crowding him. He was talking before he knew the words were leaving his lips. "I know a few other things, too, miss. I know that—"

"Quinn," the woman said.

Matt stopped. "Pardon?"

"You said 'Miss.' I thought I'd square the

record. Give you the name you didn't know. I'm Miss Quinn. Or you can call me Jessie."

"Miss Quinn."

The dark eyes sparkled. "That's right. From Austin, Texas."

Matt regrouped. "Miss Quinn, I know that—"

"What's your name?" she interrupted.

Taken completely off balance, Matt stared at her.

"Your name." The young woman shook her head as if in disbelief. "You got to know your name. If you can't call it to mind right at the moment, check the back of your shirt. Maybe your momma wrote it there for you." She raised an arched brow suspiciously. "You do know how to read, don't you?"

"I read fine," Matt responded. "And as I was saying before you interrupted me, I know that a young woman should not be down among a bunch of men unescorted like that."

"I was escorted," Jessie said.

"Then you should have stayed with your escort."

"My escort had business with the owner. He understands that I can take care of myself. And you never did give me your name."

"Forgive my friend's manners," Paul put in quickly, doffing his hat like a proper gentleman and performing an abbreviated bow. "He's not quite himself this morning."

"I'd hardly call this time of day mornin',"

Jessie said. "Back on the ranch in Texas, we'd already have nearly five hours of workin' the stock in by this time of day."

Paul gave Jessie their names. Matt kept silent. He felt annoyed at the young woman, but he knew it was not her fault. His anger at Creighdor was spilling over.

"A lord?" Jessie looked somewhat intrigued, but nowhere near impressed. "You look too young to be a lord. Most of the lords I've been introduced to are a lot older. Heavier an' gray-haired, too."

And how many lords and ladies have you met? Matt couldn't help wondering.

"How do I know you're not just spinnin' a tale to turn my head?" Jessie asked.

"Why would I do something like that?" Matt asked.

Jessie put a hand on her hip and rolled her eyes. "Maybe for the same reason those men thought makin' vile suggestions would appeal to me. I have found that most men, 'cept for my daddy, tend to run to stupid when they're around a pretty woman."

"You seem to have a very high regard for yourself."

She showed him a challenging smile. "I just play my cards as they're dealt. Straight up an' flat on the table. I like playin' with people who do the same. Saves time."

Matt put his hat on his head. "Miss, I have

some advice for you: In the future, I'd suggest you remain in the company of your escort."

Jessie patted her handbag. "That's funny. I was thinkin' maybe he'd be safer with me."

"Weapons aren't allowed in London," Matt said. "This is a civilized city. The most civilized city in the world. Nothing at all like . . . like Texas."

"No it isn't," Jessie responded. "I've found men here don't often keep a civil tongue in their heads." She smiled. "And I wouldn't go around talkin' about how pistols ain't allowed in London, Mr. Lord Brockton. That's kind of like the pot callin' the kettle black, don't you think? I mean, given the fact that you're carryin' two pistols, bigger than mine, in your coat pockets right now."

Matt started to deny the accusation.

Jessie held up a gloved hand and smiled again. "That's your business. An' don't bother tellin' me I was wrong. When you came up to save me, one of them bumped up against my leg. My grampa was a bandit an' a gambler, an' he taught me to look for hideout-guns an' somebody dealin' from the bottom of the deck. Didn't take me but a shake of a lamb's tail to see how your coat was hangin' straight to know that you carried a pistol in your other pocket too." She frowned. "Of course, it could be a brick. To help balance out the coat, but that would be pretty stupid, wouldn't it? Carryin' a brick when carryin' another pistol would be twice as good if you feel you have the need to carry the first one. I mean, do you go to jail any longer over here for totin' two weapons than for just totin' one?"

Looking into the dark eyes, Matt got the impression that her question was intended as serious. He didn't know what to say.

"Miss Quinn."

Glancing past the young woman, Matt saw Creighdor stepping from the glassworks entrance.

"Are these men bothering you?" Creighdor asked. "I'd heard there was some confusion down in the foundry."

A crowd had gathered round the scene, no doubt attracted by the young woman in her scandalous foreign dress. Some of those in attendance were Creighdor's men, though. Matt recognized the hard look of them inside their suits.

"Not in the slightest, Mr. Creighdor," Jessie answered in a demure tone that didn't at all match the cursing, pistol-packing young woman Matt had seen down in the foundry. "Thank you for your concern, though. They just brought me outside for a breath of fresh air."

"Perhaps you'd like to come back inside," Creighdor suggested. "I want to pick out those dishes I'm getting for your mother."

"All right." Jessie turned back to Matt and Paul. "Adios, gentlemen." She touched her hat in a two-fingered salute that was unself-conscious and not ladylike at all.

Before Matt knew what to say, Jessie turned and walked away. Creighdor held the door open and let her walk inside. As soon as the young woman was out of sight, he crossed the distance to Matt and Paul.

"I do hope this morning's exercise has been illuminating for you," Creighdor said. "You're taking part in a game that is far over your head."

Matt started to take a step forward. Creighdor never moved, but Paul placed a hand on Matt's arm and held him back.

"You're not half the man your father was, boy," Creighdor said in a low, gruff voice. "I broke him. Turned his friends and his fortune against him. How can you believe even for a moment that I can't do the same to you?"

Controlling the anger and frustration that swirled within him, Matt pushed his breath out. "You were afraid of my father. Don't forget that."

Creighdor maintained a level gaze. "Never."

"You were," Matt said. "That's why you had him murdered. You were afraid of him, and I'm going to teach you to be afraid of me."

"You're a child playing at being a man," Creighdor said. "That's why I sent you that trinket. To help you remember that." He tucked his walking stick up under his arm and pulled at his gloves. "You have something of mine. I want it back. It doesn't matter if you live or die. I'm going to get it back."

The front door to the glassworks opened. Jessie Quinn stuck her head out.

"Mr. Creighdor," she called.

Creighdor never took his black gaze from Matt. "On my way, Miss Quinn." He lowered his voice. "Soon, boy. Bring back what is mine soon. I have been generous thus far. I will get tired of waiting. Dying can be a very hard thing, and I have men in my employ who can fill the time with pain." Without another word, he turned and walked away.

Fear gripped Matt. The feeling was so strong he had to acknowledge it. His father had taught him the value of fear, that sometimes it could help a man save himself through sudden physical ability, or numb him to the horror of something he had to do in order to preserve his own life. Roger Hunter had never talked of his service in the Crimean War, but Matt had always known those were the times his father had referred to.

Creighdor had meant every threat he'd uttered. Matt wanted to attack the man and bring that challenge to a head, to confront it and be done with it, one way or the other.

"Let's go," Paul said, taking his friend by the arm and flagging down a hansom cab.

Matt allowed himself to be guided into the cab when it stopped. He sat on the bench seat and looked at Paul. "Jessie Quinn. The name sounds familiar."

"It should," Paul said as he joined him in the cab. "Her father is an American ambassador stationed here in London. The family arrived from Texas only a few days ago."

"What else do you know about her?"

Paul shook his head. "Nothing."

"We need to find out. If Creighdor is spending time with her, there has to be a reason."

"She is a very beautiful young woman."

"Yes, but would that be enough to capture Creighdor's attention?"

"I don't know." Paul rapped on the cab roof and the driver got underway.

"She is also the daughter of an American ambassador."

"America is a thriving market. We have more in common these days than we ever have. Trade has been good for both countries."

Matt nodded. "We need to know more about her."

"And her father, the ambassador."

"Yes."

"Perhaps you could ask Emma about the ambassador and his daughter."

"I'm not going to talk to Emma about this," Matt said. The cab turned the corner, heading back to Fleet Street.

"Matt, you don't have a choice. Time is working against you." Paul hesitated. "Just as it's working against you concerning your cargo ships. Gabriel has already told you that he's running out of places to hide the head. And Mr. Chaudhary has informed you that he can't figure out the device inside the skull. Matt . . ." A worried look flashed through Paul's eyes. "If we're to do this, if we're to avenge your father, if we're to stop Creighdor, you have to know when you need help."

"Risking Emma is out of the question."

Paul was silent for a moment, rolling his walking stick between his palms. "Have you given any thought to how she is going to feel about being kept out of this thing when she finds out?" He pressed on. "She is your friend. One of your best friends. She is also one of *my* best friends, and I don't want to deal with any remonstration she will direct my way. And she is in a position, on a number of fronts, to help you. Her father is chief inspector at Scotland Yard. When the time comes that you can build a case against Creighdor, who else could you go to?"

Matt sighed. Paul was right. There was no denying that.

"Emma can help us obtain information," Paul said. "Creighdor delivered a beating to us this morning." He licked his lips. "I killed a man last night to accept the planned delivery of a child's toy. We simply can't find out enough about Creighdor's operation to be effective. Emma could help."

"I know."

"And when it comes to the mysterious box inside the mummy's head, or even the animated gargoyles, Emma could probably offer elucidation there as well. She loves science."

Matt nodded. "I'll think about it."

"Do so. But don't take too long."

Chapter 6

"You brought me out here tonight to look at a dead man's head?" Emma Sharpe gazed at Matt in disbelief.

Thankfully, Matt also noticed a fair amount of interest in his childhood friend's china blue eyes. At sixteen years of age, a year younger than he, Emma was probably the most curious person he knew. She always wanted to know everything about anything.

Dusk had come and gone hours ago, leaving darkest night stretched out across the metropolis. Only street gaslamps and a few lanterns in residences broke the inky blackness. Plumes of sick gray smoke from factory stacks wound lazily through the sky.

Despite her ladylike grace and charm, Emma possessed—as she preferred to term it—the keen and inquisitive mind of a scientist. Over the past couple of years Emma had successfully dragged

Matt to a number of scientific seminars and discussions throughout London and twice to Paris across the Channel.

"Yes," Matt replied truthfully. "I am bringing you to see a dead man's head. But this isn't just any head." Even though he felt compelled to defend his decision, he regretted saying that. For a moment he felt very much as he had as a child when he and Paul had tricked Emma into looking at a particularly interesting insect or crawling thing at the Hunter family estates. During those days, Paul and he had hoped to offend her delicate feminine sensibilities.

Instead, Emma had nearly always known far more about the insects and crawling things than they had, and she could often identify them. She had picked up snakes and toads the boys had believed must be poisonous from their appearance.

Emma tugged thoughtfully on her gloves as she studied him. "You did say the head once belonged to a mummy." She stated the matter as if that fact alone excused his ill grace.

"I suppose it still does. Though I doubt very much the mummy will come calling for it."

"As in those horrid stories published in *The Strand* and some of the other magazines?" Emma smiled at him. She'd had him read some of the fanciful fictions, only to rip them apart later for their inconsistencies and lack of research.

"Yes."

"From Egypt?" Emma asked.

Matt nodded.

"I ask only because there are also mummies in South American cultures."

Matt hadn't known that, but he wasn't completely surprised that Emma did.

"Why did you bring me here?" Emma asked.

"A mummy's severed head is hardly the type of thing I would come calling with. And if your father had seen it, I don't think I would have been allowed in the house."

Emma's father, Edmund Sharpe, was a chief inspector at Scotland Yard. Even if he had allowed the head's presence at his home, his wife would not have. Mrs. Sharpe scarcely put up with her daughter's proclivities toward science and independence as it was.

"You could have come at a more reasonable hour."

"I do apologize for the lateness of the hour. Paul and I have been rather busy today."

"Paul?" Emma replied, somewhat shocked. She smiled and shook her head. "Our Paul? Involved with a mummy's head? Do you know how impossible your story suddenly sounds? I would come closer to believing one of those shocking mummy stories in *The Strand*."

"It does sound unbelievable, doesn't it?" Matt asked, grinning in spite of the tension he felt.

"Quite."

"As I said before," Matt told her, "this isn't

just any mummy's head." *No, this is the one my father was searching for. Finding out about this mummy was one of the secrets that got him killed.*

It wasn't just any mummy's head.

"You could also have picked a better location." Emma glanced meaningfully through the hansom cab's windows at the neighborhood around them.

London's East End was filled with dark and dour buildings that sat like grumpy old men along twisting streets and narrow alleys. Crimes and violence took place there on a daily basis. Theft and murder and domestic abuse challenged the police officers, who generally only tried to keep the peace during the daylight hours. Enforcing the laws at night without a small army on call was risky business.

They rode in the cab with a driver Paul had sent round for. He was a man Paul had guaranteed would stand by them should circumstances become harsh. The scars and hard look of him spoke volumes about the fact that he was no stranger to violence.

Emma wore a dark dress with a faint lacy pattern on the collar and sleeves. A small hat sat primly atop her strawberry blond hair and moonlight shimmered over her curls. She wrapped herself in a knitted shawl.

Without warning, a lithe shadow broke from the corner of a building and launched itself at their cab.

Matt reeled back at once, reaching into his coat pocket for the big Webley revolver. In the blink of an eye, Matt pointed the gun at the shadow gripping the cab's side.

"For the love of God, mate," a young voice whispered hoarsely, "don't shoot! I ain't 'ere to 'arm you none, I ain't!"

The boy clinging to the cab was no more than nine or ten. He wore ragged clothing. Dust and grime coated his pinched face.

"I've come by way of Gabriel, I 'ave," the boy went on without drawing a breath. "'E sent me, 'e did. To look after you."

Matt held the pistol on the boy.

"If'n you two weren't in danger an' I didn't 'ave orders from Gabriel 'isself, I'd let go this cab an' let 'ob take you, I would," the boy snarled, getting some of his courage back. "Get that cannon outta me face."

Matt lowered the hammer and rested the weapon in his lap. "What danger?"

"You're bein' follered."

"By whom?"

"Some blokes what works for Scanlon. I didn't wait round an' get their names. Thought there was 'ardly any need for it when we saw they was after you."

Matt started to shove his head through the cab's window.

The boy put a hand on top of Matt's head and shoved back with surprising strength.

"An' that would be right smart, wouldn't it?" The boy cursed like a sailor. "You a-lookin' out that winder right now. No, they wouldn't catch on that you know about them at all." He tugged on his cap and glanced at Emma. "Beggin' your pardon, ma'am. Didn't mean no disrespect, I didn't."

"Matt?" Emma's voice was tight.

"Everything's all right."

"You're carrying a pistol."

Matt shoved the weapon back into his coat. He decided not to mention that he was carrying *two* such pistols, as well as enough cartridges to wage a small war. "There's a need."

Emma looked at the boy. "I presume, since you warned us but did not warn us away, that you have a plan."

"Aye." The boy nodded and grinned excitedly. "We gots a trap set up for 'em. Gabriel, 'e suggested it, 'e did. Just you two be ready to move quicklike. An' don' be fearful an' such." He raised his voice. "The next alleyway to the left, driver. Suddenlike, if you please." He gripped the bill of his small leather cap, winked, and fell away from the cab.

Emma stood and gazed out the window. Matt caught her and sat her back down.

"He's awfully spry," Emma said with slight amazement. "He never lost his footing."

"Gabriel's boys have all learned to be fleet of foot." Matt didn't add that they'd learned those skills while running from the police, angry victims of their thievery, or rival gangs.

"Who might Gabriel be?"

Matt remembered then that Emma had never met Gabriel. "He's a thief."

Emma's eyebrows rose a little as she turned back to regard Matt. "You're friends with a thief?"

Matt nodded.

"Well," Emma declared, "you certainly are filled with surprises tonight."

"'Ang on," the driver advised from behind and above.

The horse suddenly bolted into a brisk trot that made the cab race along the street. Potholes jarred the vehicle. Abruptly, the horse turned at a shadow-filled alley.

Matt slid across the leather seat but caught hold of the window frame so he didn't crush Emma behind him. He peered through the window and spotted the small carriage pursuing them. That vehicle's driver was whipping the two-horse team into a faster gait. Dark lamps swayed on either side of the pursuing carriage. The faces of two men crowded the windows, but Matt felt certain he spotted the shadows of more inside.

Then the corner of the alley filled his vision. The cab plunged through the narrow lane, iron-bound wheels ringing.

A small loading area behind a warehouse rose nearly to the height of the cab's door. The metal door slid up and Matt spotted the young boys hauling on the chain inside the storage area. Other boys stood behind rows of barrels.

The carriage came around the alley corner. In just the past few seconds, it had shortened the lead held by the hansom cab.

In the next instant, barrels tumbled from the warehouse, initially just a few, then a deluge. The thunder of the heavy barrels striking the cobblestones filled the alley. The first of them landed in front of the horses, but the later arrivals smashed into the team. The big animals lost their footing and went down in heaps.

"Oh!" Emma cried. "The horses!"

Thankfully, though, the horses stood and appeared none the worse for wear. However, the carriage was mired in scattered barrels.

Six men clambered from the stalled carriage and started trying to clear the way. Their effort was no use. By the time they managed to get the barrels out of the alley, Matt and Emma would be long gone.

"Matt." Emma's voice had that tone in it, and that tone made it clear that she would no longer put up with foolishness.

Or secrets, Matt told himself. Reluctantly he sat back in the cab seat as the driver wheeled the vehicle out onto the street and through the other end of the alley.

Emma gazed at him expectantly. She had her arms crossed and one eyebrow cocked.

"Do you remember how my father was treated these past seven years?" Matt began. "How his friends deserted him when he said my mother died at the hands of conspirators? And that worse things were bound to happen?"

"Yes," Emma replied, losing a little of the sternness.

"Everything my father tried to tell people was true," Matt said. "Only it's much worse than we ever imagined. Probably worse than anything he imagined." He held the pistol between his knees, unwilling to put it away. And he began telling her the story of how Lucius Creighdor's gargoyle had killed Roger Hunter, and everything he, Paul, Gabriel, and the Chaudharys had managed to find out since.

Chapter 7

Well, it *is* a human skull." Emma held the mummy's head up in one hand, resting the object easily on her perched fingers. Her face was only inches from the mummy's. "In case there had been any question about that."

"Look at her holding that repulsive thing," Paul whispered behind his hand to Matt. He had yet to touch the mummy's head, and he probably never would. "As if she did this sort of thing every day."

"She's always said a scientist's only true tools were the hands, eyes, and mind," Matt replied. "Despite the invention of microscopes and other gadgetry, nothing has yet replaced a scientist's need to touch and observe in order to better understand."

Matt leaned against a wall inside the warehouse Paul had managed to find in their latest relocation attempt. He watched Emma, only a little surprised at her composure.

"Our Emma really is quite special, isn't she?" Paul asked with a trace of pride.

"Yes," Matt agreed. "But you know she would object to being referred to as *our* Emma. She's very much her own person, and she would set you to rights immediately over that."

Paul's smile only deepened. "Quite. I should expect she'd beat me rather soundly around the head and shoulders. Till I was properly penitent."

"Without a doubt."

"You'll note that I made the reference to you, safely out of her hearing."

"I had no questions about whether it was human, miss," Narada Chaudhary replied from the small keg of nails he was using as a seat, only a short distance from Emma. "The apparatus inside the skull was what most interested me."

Emma placed the skull on the small table in front of her. Her face was intent. "This is surprising."

"What?" Narada stepped closer.

"He had all of his teeth at the time of his death. None of the mummies I have seen, except for those of one young mother and a child, have had a full complement of teeth. I find the fact that this one has all of his fascinating. He was in exceptional health. Until he died, of course." She tapped the skull with the knife. Hollow pops sounded in response. "You sawed the braincase open?"

"Yes. I was very careful not to damage the apparatus."

"So the skull was intact when it came into your possession."

Narada said that it was.

Emma turned the flame up on the lamp sitting on the table. Full-length mirrors ringed the work area in such a manner that the light was reflected again and again, making a pool of illumination in the heart of the dark warehouse. Emma had insisted on the mirrors, which had taxed even Gabriel's talents for acquiring things. The set-up, she explained, was very much like a surgery theater and provided a tremendous amount of light.

When she'd described what she needed to do the examination, Matt had wondered how often Emma had been inside a surgery, and he thought again how much he did not know about his friend's interests.

The knife blade scraped against the yellowed bone as Emma sought the fissure Narada Chaudhary had created in the skull. The top of the skull popped off into her hand. A metallic surface gleamed inside the braincase.

Despite the fact that he had seen the apparatus a number of times over the past few days, Matt found himself drawn to the sight again. It was one of the greatest mysteries they had so far uncovered. He approached and peered quietly over Emma's shoulder.

The apparatus was the size of a small snuff box. Its surface was the greenish color of tarnished copper. The mysterious device molded to the skull's surface where it touched, but the side where it would have made contact with the brain remained harsh and edged.

"Interesting," Emma commented, as she picked the skull up again and rolled it around in her hands, examining the apparatus from all sides. "This is definitely a man-made construction. Do you know what this material is?"

"Metal of some kind, I suppose," Narada said. "This side of the device conforms to the skull."

Emma held the skull and ran the knife blade along the edge of the apparatus where it adhered to the bone. "As if it were poured into a mold." She rocked the skull meaningfully. "This mold."

"Perhaps it was poured," Paul ventured.

"Impossible," Emma declared. "Pouring molten metal into a man's head would have killed him on the spot. Then there is the fact that there was no way then to properly place such an apparatus inside the head of a living man. A man's brain occupies the full depth and breadth of his skull. That's why any injury that causes the swelling of the brain is so dangerous. There is simply no place for the brain to swell after being concussed." She withdrew the knife blade. "Even now, with as far as medicine and science have progressed, we lack the necessary tools and skills to properly deal with brain injuries."

Emma traced fine lines along the inside of the skull and down into the neck. The lines ended abruptly where Matt had sawed through the mummified flesh and bone.

"What are those?" Matt asked.

"Wires. Very fine wires. No bigger than strands of hair." Emma turned the skull over and found the stumps of the wires embedded in the bone. She raised her voice. "You say this head showed pictures, Matt?"

"Yes." The images that had radiated from the mummy's hollow eyes aboard *Saucy Lass* were burned into his memory. "Light flashed from the mummy's eyes and the images showed in the air."

"Like a magic lantern show?" Emma asked.

"No," Matt answered. "When I described that to you earlier, that was the closest thing I could compare it to. And a magic lantern has to have a surface on which to shine. There was no such surface under the images the mummy projected."

Magic lantern shows, which toured the country, were entertainments in which candle-powered projectors threw specially prepared pictures onto walls and ceilings while story-tellers entertained with narrative.

"In addition, the images I saw weren't flat like those you see at a magic lantern show." Matt saw the images of shifting sands and people and pyramids again. "They were more real. Raised instead of flat. They looked like I could walk into them."

"Three-dimensional instead of two-dimensional, you mean?"

"Yes. And there was motion. The people I saw . . . moved. The people walked and talked, as if I were standing there observing them."

Emma used the point of the knife to dig at the fossilized bone surrounding the wires. Tiny pieces of ivory came away and revealed more of the wires. A small pile clustered on the table in front of her.

"Did the wires continue down into the mummy's body?" Emma asked.

"I didn't notice."

Emma kept working for a moment, putting her thoughts together. "I think another apparatus inside the mummy's body provided the power to operate this one. The device in the skull must be the . . ." She frowned. "*Magic lantern*, for lack of a better term."

"Are we going to need the mummy's body to make this device work?" Matt asked.

"I don't know." Emma looked at Narada. "Please hand me that battery."

Gabriel had brought the battery when he'd brought the mirrors. The battery was big and bulky, weighing over three pounds. At this late hour, with no place to purchase one, Matt knew that a wealthy individual was missing a battery for his doorbell, or that one of the telegraph offices along the Thames River was missing a battery. Those were the only uses most of London had found for batteries.

Working carefully, Emma braided extra copper wire to the wires she'd exposed in the skull. She attached one of the elongated wires to a battery post, then reached for the second. The instant she touched the remaining wire to the second post, green light blazed in the mummy's hollow eyes.

Narada and Paul drew back at once. Paul twisted the head of his walking stick and bared the sword hidden inside. The green light was so bright it made even the reflected lamplight seem dim.

Through it all, Emma remained calm. She balanced the skull in one hand while she held the wire to the battery with the other.

An image formed in the air almost three feet from the skull. Just as on *Saucy Lass*, the images moved, but the scene barely flickered into existence before the light died.

"Egypt again?" Emma asked.

"Judging from the pyramids shown in that brief view," Paul responded, "I'd say that was the case."

Emma tried the connection again but nothing happened. She examined the battery briefly. "All the power has gone out of it."

"Another battery, then?" Paul asked.

Emma frowned. "We need something much

more powerful. A generator, I should think. At the very least."

"What do you suppose it is?" Matt asked.

Rotating the skull in her hands, Emma countered with, "What do *you* think it is?"

"A recording device."

"I concur. Do you know where the rest of the mummy's body is?"

"Creighdor might still have it."

"You said the ship sank suddenly."

"Yes, the vessel is now at the bottom of the Thames. Creighdor has had salvagers looking for it, but Gabriel's spies say they haven't found anything yet."

A cautious thump hit the top of the warehouse roof, followed quickly by another.

The sound drew Matt's attention. He stared up into the dark shadows that lay beyond the nimbus of light created by the mirrors and lanterns. The thumps sounded like large, ungainly birds had alighted on the warehouse. He reached into his coat pockets for his pistols.

Narada rose from the keg of nails, dusted his hands over his leather apron, and took up the nearby rifle.

"Matt?" Emma whispered.

Things walked across the warehouse roof.

"Paul," Matt said softly, "see to Emma's safety."

Instantly, Paul crossed the distance to Emma. He raised the glass on the lamp and blew out the flame. Orange embers clung to the wick, reflected hundreds of times in the surrounding mirrors. Lanterns at either end of the warehouse provided a small relief from the gloom that settled over the warehouse's interior.

Heavy footsteps echoed across the roof.

"Which way?" Paul asked.

"To the rear," Matt said. "Quickly."

Chaudhary scooped the mummy's head into a small burlap bag, then trailed after Paul and Emma.

Listening to the furtive footsteps, Matt cursed himself. *I should not have brought Emma into this. I knew better!* Now he prayed that he'd be able to get her safely out of the mess.

Chapter 8

Matt led the way through the stacks of crates and barrels. The others followed. They neared the rear of the warehouse and Matt's vision cleared as he got used to the lack of light. He fisted the Webleys at his sides.

Paul stepped in front of Emma, slid the lock-bar from the door, and pulled it open.

The ever-present musk of the river and the factories pushed into the warehouse in a rush. And something else shoved into the warehouse as well.

The gargoyle stood only five feet tall, but the impossible creature was almost as broad across with the leathery-looking batwings that grew out of its shoulders. Its face was a hideous nightmare: snarling fangs, gaping maw, and eyebrows sharp as razorblades. Three horns jutted up, two from its forehead and one from its broad nose. It was charcoal gray from accumulated grime, and splattered with bird droppings. Malevolent green light, so much like the light that had spewed from the mummy's eye hollows, glinted in its gaze.

Paul tried to slam the door shut again. Before he could close it, the gargoyle thrust its arm into the opening. Claws raked the air.

"Back," Matt ordered.

Paul caught Emma and pulled her backward.

Matt raised both Webleys before him as he stepped in front of his friends. He pulled the hammers back, lessening the trigger pull required to fire the pistols.

The gargoyle, eerily silent throughout the attack, slapped the door open. Hinges gave and the door sagged inside.

As soon as the evil face came into view, Matt fired. The weapons jumped in his hands, and he eared the hammers back again as the muzzle flashes filled the darkness for a split second like lightning.

Both heavy .455 bullets caught the gargoyle in the face. Matt fired again immediately, adjusting his aim and pulling smoothly through the revolvers' double-actions.

The gargoyle's head went to pieces. Chunks of stone slapped against the walls surrounding the door and sped outside. Sparks jumped on the wiring revealed in the gargoyle's broken head. Half its sneering face was missing. As if drunken or crippled, the thing lurched into the warehouse with its hands outstretched. Bullets had passed through one of the batwings, leaving only a broken stump behind.

Shifting his aim again, Matt put two more rounds through the leg the gargoyle stepped forward with. The limb shattered. The gargoyle fell forward on the stump. The green light in its eyes died.

"Move!" Matt yelled. He wasn't surprised to hear his voice crack a little. Even though he'd confronted the gargoyles three times before, he still found the experience unnerving. "After me!"

Matt rushed through the door, holding the pistols up and at the ready. Paul and Emma followed, with Narada bringing up the rear.

Steep stairs led down the back of the warehouse to the twisting alley nearly ten feet below. Matt's boots thumped against the steps. After a quick glance showed him that nothing lay ahead of him, he turned his eyes and his pistols skyward.

"Over here!" The voice of one of Gabriel's street urchins ripped out of the darkness. "Over here!"

Matt swept his gaze toward the spot the voice came from.

"Step lively!" the boy yelled. He stood at the open basement doors of the building behind the warehouse.

Paul guided Emma toward the basement

opening at once. Gabriel had versed them all on the area, and he'd taken care to explain that all of Paul's choices for working areas must be near the warrens that ran through London's underbelly. With all the construction constantly going on, the hasty tearing down of the old to build the new, tunnels and forgotten areas threaded underneath the city. Most petty criminals had learned those passages as a means to get away from law enforcement.

A shadow suddenly appeared at the peak of the warehouse roof. For an instant the gargoyle showed stark and monstrous against the sliver of moon showing in the smoky heavens. Then the creature dived, its wings spreading as it took flight.

Matt fired his remaining three shots steadily. Narada's rifle roared beside him. Out on the river and from nearby warehouses, night watchmen and sailors rang alarm bells.

Broken pieces sailed from the gargoyle. A shower of sparks rained from its head. In an abrupt end to its flight, the gargoyle smashed against the side of the building and dropped in a broken heap.

Shoving one of his empty revolvers into his coat pocket, Matt broke the other weapon open and started reloading. He raced to the basement, watching in disbelief as Emma fought her way clear of Paul and doubled back to the gargoyle.

"There are more," Narada said, reloading his rifle. The burlap bag containing the mummy's skull hung from his belt, thudding against his thigh.

"Emma," Matt called.

"A moment." Emma reached into the broken head of the gargoyle and grabbed one of the metal boxes. Sparks erupted as she pulled the device away, but these quickly died. Emma cried out and dropped her prize, and from her reaction Matt deduced that it was hot. She tried again, using the hem of her dress to seize it this time just as Paul caught her arm and hauled her down into the basement.

Matt and Narada Chaudhary went through the basement entrance together. Three of Gabriel's lads quickly slid home lockbars behind them. The escape routes, as always, had been set up prior to the meeting.

"'Astily, 'astily," one of the boys said. "Quick as you can. Them doors ain't gonna 'old those things out forever, they ain't." He turned up the flame on a lantern he carried, just enough that the shadows retreated somewhat, and jumped into motion. "Come along now. Quick as you can. We can lose them things, we can."

Pounding sounded against the closed basement doors, letting Matt know the automatons hadn't given up their hunt. *How much do they think on their own? Or do they merely follow prescribed instructions?*

He shoved his loaded pistol back into his coat pocket, then took out the other and loaded it while following the twisting paths under the city. He raced up beside Emma.

"Everything you told me was true, wasn't it?" she asked a little breathlessly. Strands of blond hair hung in her face.

"Yes," he said.

"I mean, I believed you, of course. Because you are my friend and because I held the mummy's head myself. But . . ." Words failed her.

"It's all right." Matt clicked the second pistol closed. He pointed at the device in Emma's hand, still wrapped in her dress. "You can't keep that."

"There is much I can learn if I'm allowed to examine this," she protested.

"Creighdor might be able to trace that more easily than he can trace the mummy's head," Matt said. "I know he and his men control the gargoyles in some fashion. It is too much of a risk." He took the device from her hands, feeling her reluctance, then cast it aside.

Behind them, the thumping against the closed basement doors continued. For good or ill, Matt knew Emma was involved. Even if Creighdor wasn't aware of her involvement, Matt knew that he'd never be able to keep his friend out of the affair now.

He just hoped the basement doors would hold long enough for them to finish getting away.

"Did you get Emma home safely last night?" Paul sat on the other side of the hansom cab.

"Yes," Matt answered. He felt restless and fidgety. He hadn't slept well the night before. At the moment he was renting a flat in the East End under another name so Gabriel's boys could watch over him.

Paul had seen to hiding the head, continuing to pass it along to another group of Gabriel's lads, who kept it moving throughout the city and through the docks. Matt hated the risk the boys were taking by ferrying the head about, but there was no other way to safely keep it from Creighdor's lackeys.

"She had questions, I suppose?" Paul asked.

"Thousands."

Paul smiled at that, then looked instantly more sober. "She could mention all of this to her father, you know."

"She won't."

"What makes you so certain?"

"If Mrs. Sharpe discovers the risks Emma took last night, she won't be allowed out of the house for some time."

Paul grimaced. "That would also mean that your part—and mine—in the whole affair would come to light. That would not be a good thing."

"No," Matt agreed. "Chief Inspector Sharpe has a file on Creighdor."

Paul's eyebrows lifted. "A file? How intriguing. And why does a Scotland Yard inspector have a file on Lucius Creighdor?"

"Emma doesn't know. Yet."

"I thought in her capacity as her father's assistant that Emma was privy to everything."

Although her mother wanted her to stay home and help with the younger Sharpe children, Emma had managed to talk her father into championing her. As a result, she held a very "unofficial" capacity as assistant to her father regarding police matters.

"Apparently there are some things her father has seen fit to keep even from her," Matt replied.

"Is Emma going to sneak this file?"

"I don't know. She is quite torn. There are some files her father has asked her to have nothing to do with. She has always respected his wishes. But now, what she doesn't know could be quite lethal."

"To us."

"She knows that. She was the one who mentioned that fact." Matt looked out the cab's window. He recognized the neighborhood as Spitalfield, one of London's rougher districts. "What are we doing here?"

A sour smile twisted Paul's mouth. "We've come to see an acquaintance of mine."

Matt looked at the dilapidated houses. "You know someone who lives here?"

"I know someone who is in hiding here," Paul corrected. "Nigel Kirkland. Do you know him?"

"No."

"Nigel has, in the past, been a friend. However,

recently he betrayed me. He helped me gather information on potential cargoes for Hunter Shipping. He had every opportunity to know what I had planned when it came to Pender Glassworks. He's the only one who could have betrayed us to Creighdor."

"Did you come here to even the score with Nigel?" Matt had never seen Paul in a vengeful mood before.

"No. That's never been my way. But I had to ask myself how Creighdor could find a shipping line that would be able to take business out of our hands and be vulnerable to his predations." Paul spread his hands and smiled again. "Since I had no answers, I thought we might ask Nigel."

A few minutes later Matt debarked the hansom cab and looked around the squalid Spitalfield neighborhood. Only a few flats had lighted windows, mute testimony that many living in the area could not afford oil or candle.

Paul paid the driver and joined Matt.

"How did you get the address?" Matt asked as he fell into step with his friend.

"Gabriel discovered it for me." Paul led the way up rickety stairs covered with refuse. Body odor combined with the stench of urine and rotting vegetables. People slept outside the doors to some of the flats, either locked out or by choice because the rooms were overflowing. The poor lived there, Matt knew, and most of them barely eked out enough to get by. He felt vulnerable. If some of the rough men who inhabited the area saw Paul and him, there was a good chance they would try to rob them and perhaps leave their bodies in one of the alleys or the river.

A guttering candle at the end of the hallway barely illuminated the fourth-floor hallway. Paul struck a lucifer and began checking door numbers. He was on his third match when he found the one he wanted. He dropped the spent match to the floor and knocked.

"Who is it?" a thick voice demanded.

"Nigel," Paul called. "Open the door."

"Paul?" Surprise strained the voice.

"Yes. Open the door."

Cursing came from inside the flat. "Go 'way. Don't want to talk to you."

"We're going to talk."

"I've a shotgun and I *will* use it."

"Open the door, Nigel. I know what you did. I know you betrayed me. We need to talk."

"Sod off, Paul. I don't feel like talking."

"Losing an arrangement I worked hard for is my business." Paul rapped his walking stick against the stained and scarred door. "I'm not going away without first speaking with you."

Silence filled the hallway, then voices in other rooms echoed, frantic whispers and children crying.

A moment later the door opened, pulling inward only a few scant inches till it reached the end of a security chain. A shotgun barrel shoved through the door opening.

"I warned you, Paul. Truly I did."

Chapter 9

Grabbing the shotgun in both hands, Matt yanked the weapon and its wielder forward, angling the barrel upward. The shotgun roared, filling the hallway with sound and muzzle flash. Birdshot peppered the ceiling tile, breaking a section as big as a pie plate into pieces that rained down over Matt and Paul.

The barrel turned hot in Matt's hands but he didn't release it. He yanked on the weapon again. Nigel Kirkland slammed against the door. Before the man could let go of the weapon, Matt kicked the door.

The door hammered Kirkland, driving him back, then reached the end of the security chain and pulled the screws through the wood with banshee screeches.

Without pause Matt held onto the shotgun and drew a pistol from his coat pocket. He followed the Webley through the door.

A pair of candles under glass illuminated the small flat. Stains marked the walls, and the furniture had seen better days.

Nigel Kirkland, heir to Lord Pawlton, sprawled on the floor with a bloody mouth and a cut over one eye. He was lean and sallow. Dark rings underscored his feverish gaze. Holding a hand up in front of him, he said, "Don't shoot me! Please don't shoot me!"

Briefly checking the shotgun and finding it was a single-shot, Matt tossed the weapon aside. He kept the pistol trained on Nigel.

"Stay there," Matt ordered.

"I will," Nigel said in a quavering voice, "I will. I am." Lying prone on the floor, he lifted both hands in front of his face as if that would protect him from a bullet.

Striding beyond the terrified young man, Matt surveyed the flat. "Is anyone else here with you?"

"No. No one." Nigel looked desperately at Paul. "Please tell him I didn't mean to hurt anyone, Paul. The shotgun only went off because he grabbed it."

Matt knelt quickly and went through Nigel's pockets. Only a few quid, some coins, and a blue bottle of pink pills with a Dr. James Dorrance's name on it came to hand. He dropped the items on the floor.

Satisfied that Nigel was alone, Matt returned to the doorway. He hid the pistol in the folds of his coat as he stepped out into the hallway.

Several residents stood at either end of the hallway. Three of them held lamps, bathing him in light.

"Go back to your beds," Matt commanded in a harsh voice.

"Will there be any more shootin'?" a man asked.

Matt turned to address the speaker, unable to see him for the lamp in his hand. "This business belongs to us. If you don't go back to your rooms this minute, I'll pull in a squad of men and have all stragglers in jail by morning."

"Scotland Yard," someone said.

"An inspector," someone else muttered.

"What do they got to come down 'ere for? Ain't no crimes bein' done 'ere."

Without a word the crowd dispersed.

Matt knew that his attire had convinced them he was a Scotland Yard inspector, or—at the very least—a gentleman of means. Lower class did not clash with upper class, and for once he was glad of the separation instead of being embarrassed and uncertain about it. His father had talked to all men as his equals, and Matt had never abused the different stations the fates had separated men into. He felt bad about the ruse, knowing that his appearance would frighten a number of the residents for days to come.

"Well," Paul said as Matt returned to the room, "that went better than I expected. I thought you would surely get shot."

"You aren't a Scotland Yard inspector," Nigel accused. He wiped at his bloody mouth.

Anger spilled over inside Matt. He reached down and one-handed Nigel to his feet. The young man didn't put up a fight. Matt shoved Nigel into the tattered chair against the wall.

"You can't do anything to me," Nigel said.

Matt slapped him with an open hand.

Nigel's eyes went wide and he ducked under his arms.

"You could have killed my friend," Matt said. "I should kill you for that alone." He hated how easily the anger and violence rose up in him. During the last seven years he'd become more and more aware of those feelings. While carousing at night, getting into fights had gotten easier.

"Paul," Nigel squealed.

Calmly, Paul sat on the corner of the small desk tucked into one corner of the room. "I can't stop him once he gets started." He reached down and picked up the long-stemmed pipe sitting in the ashtray on the desk. "Opium?"

Then Matt recognized the sickly sweet smell in the room. London had opium dens scattered throughout the underworld. The deadly, addictive drug had been grown in India by British merchants and then sold to the Chinese by force, but it had made its way back into England as well.

Paul dropped the pipe and the drug into an overflowing wastebasket by the desk. "Truly a nasty habit. You do know that it eventually kills most of those who use it, don't you?"

"What do you want?" Nigel asked. He grimaced in pain and pulled at his left ear. Matt thought maybe he'd injured the ear when he'd been pulled into the door.

"Answers," Matt said in a hard voice.

"The police will be here any moment," said Nigel, trying to sound defiant. "The *real* police."

Matt slapped the young man again, causing him to bleat in pain. "I have all the time here that I want," he stated gruffly, "but I don't want to be here any longer than I have to be."

"I'd answer his questions," Paul recommended.

Cowering in his chair, Nigel asked, "What questions?"

"You told Creighdor about the negotiations Paul had initiated with Jonathan Pender," Matt accused.

"I didn't," Nigel said, holding his face. "There's only one way Creighdor could have discovered the business Paul was setting up with. There's a man . . . a man I owe money to. A lot of money. He sent thugs round after me, and I couldn't get away. They took me to him. I thought they were going to break my thumbs or my knees, or maybe even kill me. Instead, he asked me what I knew about *you*. About your business."

"Why would he ask that?" Matt asked.

"I don't know." Ducking his head, his face

wracked with pain, Nigel pulled at his left ear again. He reached for the pills on the floor in front of him, shook two out of the blue bottle, and swallowed them. "Headaches. I have headaches all the time. Dr. Dorrance tells me it's from stress."

"You told this man about my business?" Paul demanded.

After a short hesitation, Nigel said, "Yes. Forgive me, Paul, but I did. I didn't see any way he could harm what you were doing. Or even why. He told me he would give me more time on the money I owed him if I would fess up." Nigel wept openly. "You'd have done the same thing if you'd had men standing there waiting to cut your throat. I swear you would have."

Paul shook his head in disgust. "I'd never have been standing in that man's office."

"How did Creighdor find out?" Matt asked.

"This man," Nigel said, "he works for Creighdor."

Looking completely at ease, Paul said, "I'll have the name of the man you took the loan from."

"His name is Edwin Locke," Nigel said. "Down on the docks, he's sometimes called Red Eddie."

Paul stood up from the desk and straightened his jacket. "Well then, I think we're finished here."

Nigel didn't try to get up. "Stay away from him, Paul. I'm warning you. Red Eddie is dangerous. He's a blackguard and a murderer. He'll think nothing at all of snuffing out your life like a candle. And Lucius Creighdor? He's even worse. The man is a fiend."

"I'll keep that in mind, Nigel." Paul walked from the room without a backward glance.

"I'll give you something to think on after we've gone," Matt said grimly. "If you tell Red Eddie that we had this conversation, you and I will talk again. And things won't go this well the next time. I found you once. I'll find you again if I need to."

"Red Eddie is a bad 'un," Gabriel said in a low voice. "Carries a straight-edge razor, 'e does, an' likes to use it on them what angers 'im."

Matt knelt on a stairway landing with a spyglass to his eye. Paul and Gabriel were with him. Fog from the river blew over them, masking them from any onlookers below.

Across the street, Edwin Locke stood in a narrow alleyway talking to a group of men gathered around the back of a cargo wagon. Another group of men stood at Locke's back, watching over him.

Locke was a small man, delicate boned and dapper. In his early forties, he had thinning dirty-blond hair that he kept pushed back and a thick mustache and side-whiskers that bisected his face.

His narrow, close-set eyes made his protruding nose and bony chin more prominent. He pulled at his left ear from time to time.

After leaving Nigel Kirkland, Matt and Paul had gotten word to Gabriel through his street rats. Gabriel hadn't been happy about finding Edwin Locke, but he'd done it a day later.

"Those men are his bodyguards?" Matt moved the spyglass over the men standing behind Locke.

"Yes," Gabriel answered. "Four of 'em. With 'im at every turn, they are. They get up when 'imself gets up, an' they go where 'imself goes. All of 'em are dangerous men. Got bodies tucked into sewers round the city what's got their bullets an' knives in 'em."

Matt centered the spyglass over Locke again. The man pointed to some of the crates and barrels in the back of the wagon. In addition to money-lending, bookmaking, and smuggling, Locke also fenced stolen goods.

"Perhaps we could bargain with him," Paul suggested.

"For information against Lucius Creighdor?" Gabriel shook his head. "Not bloody likely."

"Creighdor bought him. Perhaps we could as well."

"Problem with somebody like Red Eddie," Gabriel said, "is 'e don't stay bought. No, what keeps 'im clean with Creighdor is that 'e's afraid of Creighdor."

"Then we'll teach him to be afraid of us," Matt said.

"'E's comin'. 'Is bodyguards are with 'im." Gabriel looked away from the window of the hansom cab and glanced at Matt. Dark night gathered around them in the alley where they hid. "Are you ready?"

Matt gave a tight nod. His stomach churned. Finding their quarry had proven difficult. Two days had passed since they'd started chasing Edwin Locke. During that time, the man hadn't left the flat he kept off Cheapside where he lived. Tonight, though, he'd come to a physician's office in Southwark, remaining inside only a short time. Matt and Gabriel had barely gotten the cab in position before Locke reappeared.

Gabriel's plan turned out to be incredibly simple—and risky. Still, Matt knew they had no choice if they wanted to question Locke. Most of Creighdor's inner circle were unknown. Matt had Josiah Scanlon's name from the night he'd gone with his father to discover the ketch, *Saucy Lass*, and the grisly cargo the ship had ultimately yielded.

Reaching up, Gabriel tapped on the cab top with the butt of his shotgun. Dressed in black, his face covered with lampblack, he looked like a ghostly apparition.

The hansom cab shot forward, pulling out of the alley across from the doctor's office where

Locke had been. A simple brass plaque screwed to the wall beside the door announced the presence of barristers Graham and Green, and physicians Tuttle and Dorrance.

A stray thought niggled at the back of Matt's mind, something he felt he should recognize. But he was so fatigued he could scarcely keep his thoughts together. There had been precious little time for rest while they'd gotten everything ready for their foray into Locke's abduction.

The horses' hooves clopped against the cobblestones, the noise ringing out over the quiet street.

Who visits a physician's office at eleven o' clock at night? Matt wondered. *Wouldn't a physician come to someone's house rather than having a patient come to him?*

"E'ening, guv'nor," the hack driver said as he pulled the hansom cab to a stop in front of Locke. "Would you like a ride somewheres?"

"No," Locke growled.

"*Now,*" Gabriel said, leaning forward to open the cab door. He thrust the shotgun through the door as Matt shoved both pistols through the window.

Locke froze and stared at the shotgun barrel only three feet from his face.

"At this range," Gabriel said coldly, "it'll make quite the mess, I'm afraid."

Chapter 10

Edwin Locke's four bodyguards stood flat-footed in the dim glow of the gaslight on the street corner. They stared up at Matt's pistols thrust through the cab's window. If the men had weapons on their persons, and Matt had every reason to believe that they did, they chose not to reach for them.

"What is this?" Locke demanded. "Do you know who I am?"

"I know you all right, Red Eddie," Gabriel said in a mocking tone. "You an' me, we got a bit o' business." The young thief reached to the floor of the cab for the coil of rope and flipped a noose over Locke's head. The other end was secured to the window frame on the opposite side of the cab. Gabriel jerked the rope tight round the moneylender's neck, then slammed the shotgun's butt against the cab's roof.

Heeding the prearranged signal immediately, the driver put his animal into motion.

The noose tightened around Locke's neck. The little man was barely able to hook his thumbs under the rope as he was yanked forward.

The bodyguards started to give chase. Matt fired two shots over their heads and watched as all four men dove to the ground.

Locke screamed curses, ordering Gabriel to stop the cab. He struggled to keep up while at nearly a dead run beside the cab. His efforts at loosening the knot in the noose failed.

Gabriel yanked on the rope. "Even if you get off that rope," the thief warned, "you won't get far. My friend will kill you. 'E's a dead shot, 'e is."

Locke stumbled through a pothole in the alley, barely able to keep his feet.

"An' if you fall," Gabriel warned, "we won't stop. I'll keep this cab goin' till you're dragged dead an' not an inch of skin is left on you. Then I'll cut your body loose an' let the corpse takers 'ave you for the medical schools to cut up."

"Why?" Locke gasped. He stumbled again and nearly went headlong.

"We're askin' the questions," Gabriel replied. He pulled the rope. "Now, are you walkin', or are you gonna ride?"

Locke gained the doorway, put his hands to either side, and tried to haul himself aboard. He lacked the strength, though, and fell. His chin struck the floor of the cab with a resounding thud. Gabriel caught the moneylender by the coat sleeve before he could slip under the cab's rear wheel.

"Matt," Gabriel called out.

Shoving one of his pistols into his coat pocket, Matt stood and leaned out to grasp the back of Locke's coat. He put his strength into the effort and hauled the little man bodily into the cab. Matt glanced back at Locke's bodyguards, now in the distance.

Locke lay on his back in the floor of the cab. He coughed and gagged, fighting the noose around his neck, barely able to get enough room to draw a deep breath. "I'll kill you!" His voice was a hoarse rasp.

Gabriel put the shotgun's barrel against the man's forehead. "Not tonight."

"Locke isn't going to talk," Paul said.

Standing a short distance away from where Edwin Locke sat tied to a chair, Matt felt frustrated. They had spent almost an hour questioning the moneylender, but he hadn't spilled any secrets about Lucius Creighdor. However, he had promised death and dismemberment on several occasions.

The warehouse Gabriel had chosen and broken into for the encounter guaranteed privacy for hours. The watchman overseeing security on the building was lax, and Gabriel had the man's rounds timed.

"I know." Matt glanced down at the table where they had spread out the personal belongings they'd found on Locke at the time of his capture. Money, papers, and coins shared space with cigars, a tie tack, men's cufflinks, four rings, a gold necklace, nail clippers, a pocket watch, a comb, a blue bottle of pills, and a straight razor that looked positively lethal.

Gabriel smiled a crooked smile. "Despite 'is successes as a moneylender, Locke 'asn't been able to give up 'is small-minded ways."

"What do you mean?" Matt asked.

Running a hand through the objects lying on the table, Gabriel said, "The man's a dip. Can't keep 'is 'ands out of other people's pockets, is what I mean. Most of this stuff 'ere, 'e nicked it. Prolly while 'e was out an' about tonight."

"How do you know that?"

"This stuff 'ere?" Gabriel shook his head. "It ain't all 'is own. You ever seen a bloke carryin' round a woman's necklace?"

"Maybe he's got a lady friend."

"Would you take it to 'er without a proper box an' wrap?"

"No."

Gabriel picked up the necklace and threaded it through his fingers. "No, I reckon the next place this was 'eaded was to a pawn shop. Or maybe a strumpet if Locke was of a mind for that." He put the necklace down and picked up the rings, the cufflinks, and the tie tack. "Don't figure on 'imself carryin' extra jewelry about neither."

"The nail clippers." Paul tapped the tool. "Locke doesn't need nail clippers. His own are chewed off."

Gabriel nodded. "I saw that. Good eye." He picked up the pocket watch. "Means this ain't 'is either. Them rings, that necklace an' that tie tack, I figure on takin' 'em for my troubles tonight. They'll feed some of the lads an' keep 'em off the streets."

Matt picked up a small leather-bound journal. Cryptic numbers were written on the pages inside.

"That's Locke's record book," Gabriel said. "'E keeps notes on them what owes 'im money. 'Ow much they owe, payments they've made, when more payments are due. That kind of thing."

"Knowing the names of the people he's dealing with might give us more leads to Creighdor." Matt stared at the columns of figures.

"Even if we could break whatever code he's using," Paul said, "we couldn't hope to learn all the names."

"Most of 'em's gonna be people what lives in an' round the docks," Gabriel stated. "That's where 'e does most of 'is business."

Locke was rubbing his left ear on his shoulder

when Matt approached him. Pain showed in the thin man's face. He scowled and spat when he saw Matt, but he was careful not to spit on Matt. Locke had tried that earlier and had gotten his head bagged in burlap by Gabriel. His face still showed dirt.

"There's people out lookin' for me," Locke threatened. "You know there is."

"Well, then," Matt said amiably, "it appears that they've looked all this time and haven't found you yet. Either they're not very good at it or they aren't looking as hard as you hope."

Foul curses spewed from Locke's mouth.

Taking a lead-shot-filled sap from his pocket, Gabriel rapped Locke sharply on the kneecap. The blow didn't break anything but was just hard enough to reinforce Locke's helpless state.

Matt wished there were another way to find out what he needed to know about Creighdor, but he knew there wasn't. He was up against harsh circumstances, and those harsh circumstances dictated equally harsh measures.

"Quiet down," Gabriel admonished. "Unless you want another smack."

Gritting his teeth, Locke quieted. Then he shivered all over and vigorously rubbed his left ear against his shoulder. Green fluid trickled from the ear and smeared across the top of his coat.

"I don't have a lot of time anymore," Matt said in an even voice.

"You got less time than you think." Locke's left eyelid fluttered in pain. "Creighdor will do for you, 'e will. You shouldn't ever 'ave crossed 'im."

"You're working with Creighdor."

"That was nuffink. I don't work for 'im. I was just doin' a bit o' business."

"Business?"

Locke nodded. "I'm in a business what sells information. I knew Creighdor would want to know what you was up to." The moneylender grinned evilly. "'E sure put the kibosh to your plans, didn't 'e? I 'eard about it. Took the wind right from your sails, 'e did." He laughed, but the effort was cut short by a paroxysm of pain that blanched his features. Again he rubbed his ear on his shoulder.

"What's wrong with you?" Matt asked.

"Bad ear," Locke grunted. "Got a bit of a cold in it, that's all." He nodded back at the table. "I got pills over there what will help cut the pain an' the spasms. They's in a blue bottle."

"Not till you answer some questions."

"Bleedin' 'ell!" Locke exploded. "My bloody head feels like it's about to come apart! I can't even think straight!"

Matt hardened himself against the man's obvious distress, and he made himself remember everything he'd done to Nigel Kirkland to get this far, and what was at stake. "You don't need to think. Just answer my questions."

"What do you want to know?" Locke asked.

"What business do you have with Lucius Creighdor?" Matt asked.

"Creighdor 'as been buying paper off me," Locke answered.

"Paper?" Matt repeated.

"Promissory notes," Gabriel said. "From people Locke 'as lent money to what 'asn't paid all of it back yet."

Locke nodded gingerly. His complexion was even more pale, his pupils were pinpricks. There was no doubt he was in considerable pain. "Right. Notes I 'ad from other business. Creighdor bought paper on lords an' businessmen. 'E come sniffin' round for 'em. 'E knew I 'ad 'em."

"How?"

Shivering, Locke rubbed his ear against his shoulder. The green fluid had created a large mess. "'E's been buyin' paper up from other lenders. Figured 'e'd get around to me eventually. I just let the right people know what it was I 'ad."

"What does Creighdor want the promissory notes for?"

Locke laughed. "Why, to get the money, of course. I'm owed quite a bit, I am."

"Whose promissory notes did Creighdor buy?" Matt asked. It didn't make sense that Creighdor wouldn't have an agenda.

Locke shook his head. "Now you're askin' questions that could leave me a dead man."

"Nobody," Gabriel said in a soft voice, "mentioned anythin' about you leavin' this place of a piece, did they now?"

For a moment fear touched Locke's face. Then pain seized him and caused his head to shake violently. A minute passed before the seizure ceased.

Locke raked in a hoarse gasp of air. "My medicine. I got to 'ave it."

Matt walked to the table and took up the blue bottle of pills. He stopped in front of Locke and shook the bottle.

"Give them to me. Two. I need two." Locke opened his mouth, quivering as another wave of pain built.

Matt made himself stand strong. Maybe Locke hadn't killed his father, but he was cut from the same cloth as Creighdor.

"After," Matt said. He made a fist around the blue bottle.

Locke whined like an animal. His breath rushed in and out of his nose and mouth. He cursed, then suffered another seizure.

"All right," he choked out. "Creighdor came to me lookin' for papers on businessmen an' lords. People what 'ad things 'e wanted."

"What things?"

"Don't know for sure. 'E didn't talk about it. Not with the likes o' me. 'E considers 'imself too fine a gentleman for the likes o' me." He stopped talking suddenly. His eyes rounded in fear as he stared at something over Matt's shoulder.

A man stood in the shadows at the far end of the building. A little over six feet in height, he was slender as a dancer but gave the impression of strength. Even at this late hour, he was smooth shaven. His pale face gave away no emotion, no indication of anything that ran through his mind. His hair was dark blond and carefully cut. Flinty gray eyes bored into Matt's. His suit fit him exactly.

"Ah," the man said in a soft voice. "Young Mr. Hunter, we meet at last." Switching his attention to Paul and Gabriel, the man nodded. "And friends." A small, humorless smile twitched the man's lips. "I might have known it was you who had made away with Mr. Locke."

"Matt," Paul said, unsheathing his sword cane, "do you know this man?"

Although they had never met, Matt did know him. The anger that boiled up inside Matt left him speechless for a moment. But it did not keep him from pointing the Webley at the new arrival. "His name is Josiah Scanlon."

Scanlon touched the brim of the bowler hat he wore. He gave them a sardonic look. "A pleasure, I'm sure."

"Scanlon works for Creighdor," Matt said.

"Actually, I work *with* Mr. Creighdor," Scanlon corrected. "He just prefers a more . . . forward approach to our business. I'm comfortable in the shadows."

Matt studied Scanlon. The first time he'd seen him had been with his father when they'd gone to spy on *Saucy Lass* a couple of weeks before. During that night, Roger Hunter had shot Scanlon in the chest, but he had gotten up as if nothing had happened.

"How did you get in 'ere?" Gabriel demanded.

Scanlon kept his eyes on Matt. "If you're worried about the boys you had watching over this place, don't be concerned. I left alive the ones I encountered. I didn't wish to leave a lot of bodies scattered about. Too many questions might arise. But I feel I must tell you I've never had a problem killing a child. I've always found them easier to kill than full-grown men. You might remember that in the future." He paused theatrically. "Should you decide to continue this ill-advised conflict with us."

"Get your hands up," Matt ordered, waving the pistol.

"I don't think so," Scanlon said, smiling as if a little amused. "Mr. Creighdor still finds you . . . interesting, Mr. Hunter. Far more interesting than I do, I'm afraid. But there is the matter of your father's missing book. Mr. Creighdor is loath to destroy you before that is found. Or before we can ascertain that the second book never existed or is lost forever. I, however, do not share that interest in you or what your father may have known."

What your father may have known.

The words reverberated in Matt's mind. That was why Creighdor was so interested in Roger Hunter's book. Evidently his father had known something that even Creighdor didn't know. The realization brought Matt strength. He had more to deal with than he'd believed.

Gabriel scooped up the shotgun beside him and aimed it at Scanlon. "You can join Locke," he stated in a quiet and deadly voice. "An' if you've 'urt one of my lads, you won't walk out of this warehouse alive."

Scanlon spread his hands as he regarded Gabriel. "Another time, boy. For now I came only to deliver a message."

"What?" Matt asked.

"Oh, it's not for your ears, Mr. Hunter. It's for Mr. Locke." Scanlon smiled and demonic lights glinted in his eyes.

"Me?" Locke croaked.

"Yes, Mr. Locke," Scanlon said in a calm voice. "I need you to do something for me."

"What?"

"Die," Scanlon commanded.

Behind Matt, the moneylender screamed in agony and fear.

Chapter 11

Drawn by Locke's screams, Matt looked back at their captive.

Although held by the ropes that bound him, Locke jerked in the chair. He squealed in pain and arched his back, jerking his head from side to side so hard it looked as though he was going to snap his own neck. He bent down and doubled his arms up, reaching up to gouge at his eyes. Bloody smears tracked his face.

Gabriel cursed.

Whipping back round, Matt pointed the Webley at Scanlon. He didn't offer a warning, just shifted his aim to the man's right leg and squeezed the trigger. Even as the hammer fell, though, Scanlon was in motion. The bullet cut the air where he had stood and disappeared into the darkness filling the warehouse. Locke's hoarse screams could still be heard over the sound of the shot.

Then Gabriel's shotgun boomed. The blast narrowly missed Scanlon. White scars appeared on a stack of crates where the pellets struck.

Matt drew his other pistol as Gabriel reloaded his weapon.

"Paul," Matt said. "Help Locke." Then he was in motion, racing through the darkness after Scanlon. He weaved through the stacks of crates and barrels, heading for the entrance to the building, hoping to cut his quarry off before he reached it. Listening for the man's footsteps, he was unable to hear over Locke's screams.

Gabriel ran at Matt's heels.

What did my father know that Creighdor does not? The question hammered at Matt's mind. He pushed it away and focused on remaining alive. Scanlon could have lied about leaving any of them alive. They had already tried to kill Paul.

Like a fleet-footed ghost, Scanlon disappeared around another turn. Matt followed, running as hard as he could. A moment later he rounded another stack of crates and reached the small side door that let out into the alley beside the warehouse.

"Careful," Gabriel called.

Matt nodded and came to a stop beside the door. Common sense told him not to rush through it, even though his instincts told him that if he hurried he might yet catch Scanlon. Putting his back to the wall beside the door, he kicked it outward. He thrust the pistols forward, covering the alley, but did not see Scanlon.

"Go," Gabriel urged. "I'll watch over you."

Heart thudding in his ears, the wound in his shoulder tight and sore, Matt went forward. Outside in the alley, he looked in both directions.

Scanlon was nowhere in sight.

Gabriel cursed. "I've got to check on my lads."

"Go," Matt said. "Be careful."

Gabriel took off at a run toward the front of the warehouse.

Keeping his pistols at the ready, Matt reentered the warehouse and made his way back to where they had been holding Locke. When he saw Paul kneeling over the small man, Matt breathed a sigh of relief.

Locke lay still and splayed, looking very much like a cat that had been struck by a carriage wheel.

Paul glanced up in disbelief. "He's dead."

"He can't be dead." Matt dropped to one knee and examined Locke.

The man had torn his own eyes out, leaving gory holes. Evidently he'd hooked his fingers into his mouth as well, ripping through his lips.

"How?" Matt asked. "Even the eye wounds aren't enough to kill him."

"There was considerable blood loss," Paul pointed out.

"Not enough to kill him."

Paul shook his head. "I don't know. But he hasn't breathed since he hit the floor."

"I didn't see Scanlon shoot him with anything." Matt shoved his pistol barrel against Locke's shoulder to roll him over. He turned rather easily, spilling out into a slack sprawl.

"Nor did I. Scanlon just told Locke to die. That's when Locke started screaming. When I saw that he had stopped breathing, I cut him loose. He fell to the floor like there wasn't a bone in his body." Paul swallowed. "I think he was already dead by that time."

"You can't kill with a word," Matt argued.

"And gargoyles can't fly," Paul reminded. "Yet here we are."

Fighting the panic that rose steadily within him, Matt studied Locke.

"We need to go," Paul said. "As desolate as this place is and as late the hour, someone will have to come find out what happened eventually. It would be better if we weren't here."

"I know." Reluctantly Matt turned away from the dead man and retreated to the table where Locke's belongings lay spread out. He pocketed everything, then followed Paul out of the building.

"Lord Brockton, your guest has arrived."

Still groggy from lack of sleep and mental exhaustion, Matt glanced up and saw a waiter escorting Emma Sharpe through the tea room. At ten o'clock in the morning, the establishment already showed good business. Clientele occupied nearly half of the deep booths and tables.

"Thank you, William," Matt told the slender young waiter attending his table.

"You're welcome, your lordship." William bowed his head and waited at the table.

Matt stood and greeted Emma. She wore a sensible brown dress, every inch the young lady. William seated her, took the order for tea and biscuits, and departed.

"Thank you for coming," Matt said.

"You couldn't have kept me away," Emma declared.

"Have you had a chance to look into the latest matter?" Matt referred to the murder of Edwin Locke. Two days had passed since the confrontation with Scanlon. "The papers are calling it murder."

"So is Scotland Yard. I also have this." Emma reached into her bag and took out a journal. She placed the slim volume on the table and slid it over to Matt. "I've taken the liberty of making copies of the police reports concerning the murder. They do come through my father's office, you know. I thought you might be interested."

Opening the book, Matt studied the lines of writing. Emma had a beautiful hand. After the initial reports, all neatly ordered with references made to who had composed the original, he happened upon several sketches. All of them were of Edwin Locke and his injuries.

He tapped the drawings. "Where did you get these?"

Emma craned her head to look at the picture of Locke with his eyes gouged out. "I managed a quick peek at the corpse."

Matt was stunned. "You *what*?"

"Oh don't go on like that." Emma rolled her eyes. "I swear, you and my father are so of the opinion that a female can't handle such things. Might I remind you women midwifed births long before men decided to make a science of the craft and take it over for themselves? Most women know more about the physiology of the sexes than men do simply through rearing their own children."

Although he managed to contain himself, Matt was embarrassed by Emma's declaration. Physiology certainly wasn't a subject a young woman talked about with a man.

"What would happen if your father came across these pictures?" Matt asked.

Emma raised an eyebrow and gazed at Matt over the rim of her teacup. "Or caught me going through his private files regarding your enemy?"

"You did that?" Matt felt guilty for just an instant, then curiosity took over.

"Yes." Emma sipped her tea. "If you'd gone through the journal only a little further, you would have found copies of that information as well."

Opening the book again, Matt flipped

through the pages and found the notes from Chief Inspector Edmund Sharpe.

"There are several people mentioned in those reports," Matt said.

"I also looked up Miss Jessie Quinn, the girl you met at Pender Glassworks," Emma said. "I have put the information concerning her into the book."

"If I lost this, Emma, I wouldn't want anyone to think she was part of this mess."

"It's the price of secrets. It always has been. My father holds several, and it wears him down."

Matt wondered how his father had borne the weight of all the things he knew. *Moreover, Father, how did you carry the weight of all the things you suspected?* He turned his attention back to the book. "What did you find out about Miss Quinn?"

"Miss Quinn is not exactly a young lady," Emma said. "She grew up in Texas, on a ranch carved from inhospitable land, if you're to believe the journalists."

"I thought you held only to the facts."

"Piffle," Emma said, crossing her arms and looking put out. "The facts are that Miss Jessie Quinn was raised on a working cattle ranch. Her father, Tyrell Quinn, is a cattleman. Her mother, Luisa Martinez Quinn, is half Mexican on her father's side, and half Chiricahua Apache Indian on her mother's side."

Matt was intrigued. "The United States is

known for the diversity of its people. I suppose it is unusual to find them all in one person, though."

"Miss Quinn has participated in cow-punching—"

"She punches cattle?" Despite the odd image that summoned up, Matt could believe it. Jessie Quinn had come across as a feisty young woman. He could picture her not only punching cattle, but also knocking them out.

"No. That's just American slang. She has participated in working the cattle and going on cattle drives. Her mother is also known to do such things. Both of them have also fought cattle rustlers, Mexican bandits, and Indians by the side of the cowboys on the Quinn Rolling R Ranch." Emma sipped her tea. "Since she has been here in London, Miss Quinn has been involved in three fights and one shooting incident. That I know of. The altercation at Pender Glassworks didn't make the papers, so I'm certain there were other incidents that have gone unreported."

"Really?" Matt was amazed. But he was also even further intrigued about how she came to be associated with Lucius Creighdor.

"Miss Quinn doesn't take insult from men, apparently," Emma said. "She's fought and beaten men who accosted her three times."

"And the shooting?"

"A would-be robber up in Cheapside."

Emma wrinkled her nose in disdain. "That was when Father found out that Miss Quinn also walks the streets of London armed. He is not happy about it."

"Then why doesn't the chief inspector seize Miss Quinn's pistol?"

"Her father is an ambassador. An ambassador and his family have special dispensation while living in London. That dispensation is granted by the Queen herself."

"An intriguing young woman." Matt studied the drawing, finding that Emma had rendered Jessie Quinn almost exactly as he remembered her.

"A *dangerous* young woman, you mean." Emma paused. "I've also been told she is often in the company of Lucius Creighdor these days."

They ate their biscuits and sipped tea for a few minutes. Matt flipped through the journal again, making certain no one at the nearby booths or tables had a chance to see what he had seen.

"What are you doing there?" a man barked. "Get away from there, you little vagabond!"

Drawn by the voice, Matt glanced at the large windows, which afforded a view of the street outside. The tea room was in Cheapside, one of London's most affluent districts. The young boy, dressed in patched over rags and bearing a grimy face, who peered in with his nose pressed against the glass, looked totally out of place.

Several patrons in the tea room added their

own harsh insults to the boy, but Matt noticed that a few of the shopgirls who worked at nearby dressmakers smiled.

The boy locked eyes with Matt.

"I think you are being summoned," Emma said.

Matt nodded. "If Gabriel sent someone here to Cheapside, it must be important. If you'll excuse me?"

"Of course." Emma took the last two biscuits from the serving tray and wrapped them in a napkin. "Take these to the boy. He looks hungry."

Matt accepted the napkin, bade Emma goodbye, listened to her entreaties to be careful, and settled the bill with the waiter. By that time the maître d' had seized a broom and set himself off in pursuit of the boy.

Out on the street, Matt saw the boy easily evade the maître d's attempts to catch him. The man looked ridiculous brandishing the broom like a sword. Giving up the chase, the maître d' turned and almost ran into Matt.

"Beg forgiveness, Lord Brockton," he apologized. "Those pilfering little scamps shouldn't be allowed in this part of the city. Someone ought to make a law."

Matt held his tongue. During his carousing in the East End, he'd come to recognize that circumstance often dictated the wretched state of poverty that afflicted so many people in London, not choice.

The boy stuck his thumbs in his ears and waggled his fingers derisively, then blew a raspberry and added several colorful insults, liberally spiced with swear words. Matt grinned to himself. Gabriel certainly surrounded himself with interesting people.

In the alley Matt confronted the young urchin.

The boy doffed his hat. "Yer lordship. Sorry to be interruptin' you at tea."

"It's quite all right . . ."

"Boggs, your lordship. Ever'body just calls me Boggs."

"Well then, Boggs, you've at least earned a meal through your efforts. Why did you come up here?"

"Was Gabriel, your lordship. 'E sent me to fetch you. Said to tell you 'e found the mummy. What was left of it, anyway."

Chapter 12

The river mills around a bit," Gabriel explained. "Sometimes it takes everything out—the sewage, trash, an' all—like it's supposed to, but sometimes it fills up some of the older sewers what ain't workin' properly. Like this one."

Matt walked beside Gabriel. They shared a lantern against the dank darkness that filled the sewer. Two of Gabriel's boys pulled oars on the small boat they were using to navigate the slow-moving water filled with debris from the city overhead. Rats fled before the craft, squeaking in consternation. Matt wore a handkerchief anointed with oil of vanilla against the horrid sewer stench. The odor of decay was so thick he would have sworn he could see it.

"I 'ad lads checkin' these sewers regularly," Gabriel went on. "'Oped this might 'appen, I did. These ones, they sometimes give up small treasures now an' again. Crates an' barrels what falls off ships by accident."

"Accident?" Matt repeated.

A grin split Gabriel's dark face. "All right then, I've got an arrangement with a few blokes what works the ships an' the warehouses. Sometimes they . . . *let* things slip through their fingers. For a price. We usually fetch 'em things up here."

"But today you found the mummy."

"Yes. Might not 'ave, if we 'adn't been looking for it as we was. But some other debris from *Saucy Lass* got caught up in these channels, stirred up an' missed by them dredgers out in the river. Like I said, I 'ad 'opes." Gabriel stood in the boat and lifted the lantern. The light reflected from the dark water and filled the tunnel as they rounded the bend.

Four boys sat hunkered round a figure lying half out of the water. Two lanterns added light to the macabre scene.

Matt's throat dried as he recognized the headless corpse.

Pasebakhaenniut, Matt thought, remembering the mummy's name. Loosely translated from the Egyptian language, it meant "the star that appears in the city." According to Narada Chaudhary's research, Pasebakhaenniut had been an architect in King Ramses' reign.

The mummy had also been one of the Outsiders, a small group of people who had come into the pharoah's land from outside the city. The legend was that Pasebakhaenniut had crossed the burning desert sands on foot and had never spoken of where he had truly come from. In only a few years, he had worked himself into the pharoah's favor and into an important position.

Matt stood as the boys brought the boat in to the side of the channel with expert skill. He stepped out and approached the ghastly figure. Several of the mummy's bandages showed scorch marks where the ship had caught fire and burned.

Taking the lantern from Gabriel, Matt ducked down and examined the mummy's body more closely. Water filled the open cavity of the neck. Light gleamed from the protruding spine, making the ragged bites of the scars from the cooper's saw Matt had used show even more. Most of the bandages were loosened, and some were even missing.

"I think it 'as definitely seen better days," Gabriel commented.

Shining the light around the mummy, Matt discovered several places where rats had eaten through. Patches of the decayed flesh were missing.

"Why haven't you gotten it up out of the water?" he asked.

"It's too 'eavy. An' we couldn't get a grip so easy with all the sewer filth makin' it 'ard to 'andle." Gabriel lifted a pair of curved boat hooks in both hands. "I'll be able to fetch it up now." He handed a hook to Matt.

Callously, as if the mummy had been a piece of meat instead of something that was once human, Gabriel swept the boat hook forward and sank the curved point into the mummy's back. Matt swung his boat hook and felt it sink deeply into the sodden flesh.

Together they hauled the mummy up from the water and dragged it over to the small boat.

"What is that bloody stink?"

Glancing up from the table where Narada Chaudhary worked on the mummy, Matt saw Paul entering the basement Gabriel had found for them.

"Oh. I see you found it." Paul took a scented handkerchief from his pocket and held it over his nose and mouth. "I'll wager I can even guess *where* you found it."

Matt quickly explained the discovery, including the long trip back through the sewers and the wait they'd had till Gabriel had located a suitable place for them to conduct an examination. That had taken several hours. The time was almost four P.M.

"Are you certain that Creighdor's people can't track that thing?" Paul asked when Matt had finished.

"We found it before they did," Matt answered.

"Perhaps being submerged in the water kept Creighdor's boxes from finding it."

Narada sat patiently on a stool at the head of the table while he worked on the mummy. Water still occasionally leaked from its open neck.

"The walls of this basement are thick." Matt took a deep breath and released it. "I believe the boxes Creighdor's men are using sense only the head. Otherwise they most likely would have found the body."

"Why do you think those devices seek out only the head?"

"If Emma is correct about the device inside the mummy's head being some kind of recording apparatus, it stands to reason that it is more important than the power source inside this body."

Narada took up the short bone saw lying on the table beside the mummy. "I'll need you to hold the body down."

Pulling on a pair of thick fisherman's gloves, Matt stood at one shoulder and pushed down with both hands. "Get the other side, Paul."

Clearly not happy about the experience he was about to undergo, Paul slipped on another pair of gloves and held the mummy's other shoulder. "Whatever you're doing, it has to be fast. If it isn't, I may be sick."

Narada climbed onto the table and straddled the mummy. He placed the bone saw at its neck and started sawing. The metal teeth ripped through the millennia-old flesh.

Still on top of the mummy, Narada stuck his hands into the body and pulled back both halves of the ribcage. The dead flesh came up reluctantly, giving voice to sucking noises.

Steeling himself, Matt leaned in and brought the lantern close. The light reflected from a smooth metallic surface in the ooze inside the mummy. Together, he and Narada mopped the gunk from around the surface till they disclosed a metal box slightly longer than Matt's hand, nearly that wide, and two fingers deep. Wires ran from the device and spiraled around the spine toward the neck.

"It appears," Narada said in a strained voice, "that Miss Sharpe's conjecture about the source of power within the mummy has borne fruit."

Matt stared at the strange apparatus. "I suppose we should have Gabriel bring the head here, then."

"Send for Emma as well," Paul said.

"No," Matt replied. "She very nearly got caught with us last time."

"If you try to make the device work and fail," Paul said, "then decide to bring Emma here, you're increasing the amount of time for possible discovery. Emma will be in even more danger then."

Matt broke the eye contact. He took a deep breath. "How is it that all of these decisions come to be made by me?"

"What you fail to remember is that we all

have free will. You can ask, but that doesn't mean we will come. For all you know, Emma may turn you down."

No chance of that, Matt thought, remembering how excited and curious Emma had been in the tea room. She'd be drawn to the possibilities the complete mummy offered as surely as a moth to flame.

But what right did he have to ask her? And yet, not truly knowing the stakes Creighdor played for, he had no choice.

Before the mummy's head reached the basement, Emma arrived and began asking questions at once. Matt stood nearby and watched as Emma and Narada traced the wires in the mummy's torso together, each of them speculating on why the wire was wrapped around the spine. Then one of Gabriel's boys showed up with the head in the burlap bag.

Holding the head in one hand, knowing by touch that he had it right side up because the severed spine pressed into the middle of his palm, Matt let the burlap bag fall down around his arm, revealing the grisly trophy. The head looked a little worse for wear. Matt guessed Gabriel's boys weren't quite as careful as they might have been.

Or maybe they've had more close calls with this thing than Gabriel has mentioned.

With scarcely a thought, Emma seized the

head and carried it over to the mummy. She placed it near the body, fitting it into place in line with the shoulders.

Gabriel entered the room a moment later.

"Sorry I'm late," Gabriel whispered. His attention was instantly riveted on the mummy. "I was busy followin' up on something. It appears Creighdor 'as more than a passin' interest in a Master Geoffrey Fiske. Runs in Paul's circles, 'e does."

"I know him," Paul admitted.

"Well," Gabriel said, "we'll have to look into 'im."

"We're going to have to excise part of the neck to get the wires to meet," Emma said.

"I have a flensing knife," Narada offered.

"Capital." Emma stuck out a hand. "If you please."

"The knife is very sharp. Please be very careful, miss."

"Thank you for your concern, Mr. Chaudhary, but I've been around sharp knives all my life." Emma finished the task and handed the knife back to Narada, then leaned in and began working on the wires. "I am going to match up the wires as they are. If I knew for certain what metal the wires were made out of, I might try to bridge them with additional lengths. However, that is not at this time within our purview. Please hold the shoulders for me, Mr. Chaudhary."

Narada pinned the shoulders.

"Matt," Emma called.

"Better you than me," Paul whispered as Matt stepped forward.

"Hold the head, please," Emma requested.

Placing his gloved hands on either side of the mummy's head, Matt held it steady. He breathed through his mouth instead of his nose.

Emma tried in vain to fit both her hands through the opening the bone saw had made in the mummy's chest. Growing impatient, she popped the mummy's jaw open and snaked a hand down its throat. Although she couldn't get all of her hand inside the mouth, she was able to get what she needed. She smiled. "Ah. There we go. Shouldn't be but a moment now."

Matt watched her, totally amazed at her aplomb as she went about the horrific task.

Sparks jumped from the wires Emma held and briefly illuminated the hollows inside the mummy's open mouth and eye sockets. Then a deep green light filled the sockets and beams shot into the air.

Chapter 13

Over the mummy's chest, images took shape. Pyramids formed, then melted into rolling sand dunes. People in strange clothing and robes walked through bazaars, buildings, and burial places. But the images came too fast, overlaying each other so quickly they began to blur.

Then the images shifted, showing a group of men and women in purple uniforms. Strange machines surrounded them. A man pointed to one of the windows on the table in front of him.

Looking at the screen through the image, Matt saw a blazing comet streaking through the heavens. Then the images went black and skipped again. This time the perspective took place on a battlefield that could have been in Egypt. Men fought on foot and from two-wheeled horse-drawn chariots, using bows and curved swords and spears. At least two great armies fought and dozens of men died, cut down like wheat before a scythe.

"We are peering back into time," Narada whispered in awe.

"Three thousand years," Paul agreed. "Perhaps more."

The images sped up and blurred again. Several scenes, throne rooms as well as construction sites and ships, paraded through the air above the mummy.

"These are things Pasebakhaenniut saw," Matt said. "You were right, Emma. This is some kind of record."

"This is a log," Emma said. "Instead of keeping a journal, the man used this device to record things he saw and took part in."

"Why?"

"I don't know," Emma said. "Even more important, where did he get the apparatus to do such a thing? We still haven't mastered enough science to do this."

No one had an answer.

"But why does Creighdor want it?" Matt asked.

"The knowledge alone to build such a device is worth a fortune," Paul said.

Abruptly the scene changed. A strangely shaped craft plunged from the sky, leaving a burning trail behind it. The vessel slammed into the earth and disappeared in a cloud of dust and debris.

The image changed again, becoming a map. Then a glowing red dot formed on the map's terrain.

"A treasure map?" Gabriel breathed.

"Or the site where that strange ship crashed," Paul said.

"A *flying* ship," Emma said in wonderment. "A flying ship! That thing exists!"

"Maybe not," Matt said, feeling excitement stirring within him. "That recording, if that's what this is, is at least three thousand years old."

"But could that ship be what Creighdor is after?" Paul asked. He studied the glowing map.

Matt stepped closer to the images playing in the air above the mummy's still chest. Tentatively, he poked his fingers into the image. The hair along the back of his arm stood at attention.

"A static electricity discharge." Obviously amazed herself, Emma stuck her fingers into the image too.

Then the scene changed again, rushing past the map and showing some of the same sequences of events again. The images continued to flow, bending around their fingers and hands. The speed fluctuated, increasing and decreasing in a matter of seconds. Long periods of blackness threaded through the action.

"Gaps in the log?" Paul asked.

"Possibly," Emma admitted. "Three thousand years is a long time, and the mummy was subjected to a lot of mishandling even before you sawed its head off. The apparatus could be damaged."

A knock sounded on the door, three quick beats followed by two slow ones in the agreed-upon warning signal. Gabriel answered the door.

"They's comin'!" the boy outside the door said. He was out of breath from running. "Creighdor's blokes! They's comin'!"

"'Ave they reached the building?" Gabriel grabbed his coat and tossed Paul's to him.

"No. I reckon they still ain't got a bead on this 'ere place, but it won't be long."

Matt stepped to the end of the table and seized the mummy's head. A quick wrench freed it from the connecting wires. The green images faded from view.

"No!" Emma said, but it was too late. "You could damage one of the devices like that."

"We haven't time to be gentle," Matt said, lifting his prize.

"Time to get the 'ead movin' again," Gabriel declared, tossing Matt the burlap bag. "Don't want 'em catchin' us 'ere like fish in a barrel."

Matt dumped the head in the bag and handed it to Gabriel. The young thief took off like a shot through the back door leading out to the alley.

"What about the body?" Emma asked.

Taking hold of her elbow, Matt hustled her out the other basement door. "We leave it."

"They might find it," Emma protested.

"Better it than us."

"I don't want to lose this. There is much we can learn from it."

"I know."

"We can't use the device inside the mummy's head without the power source inside its chest. We need both."

"I know. We can't take both with us." Matt guided Emma up the steps that led to the hallway and the secondhand shop on the first floor.

"What if they find the mummy?" asked Emma.

Matt pushed open the door to the consignment shop and made his way to the front door. Darkness had fallen while they had worked. The street outside the shop was steeped in shadows.

"Then they will take it," Matt told her. "And we try to get it back at a later date. That's the best I can offer."

"We could take the device out of the mummy's torso."

"Can we?" Matt looked at her, holding her in the shadows inside the store while men with lanterns passed by outside. "I thought you said the devices were adhered to the inside of the mummy."

"They are."

"So removing the devices might harm them."

"We don't need the mummy's arms and legs to power the recording apparatus," Emma replied.

Matt looked at Emma as if he'd never seen her

before. He couldn't believe she had suggested what she had in such a calm manner. Then he glanced at Paul, who was shaking his head in disbelief.

"Oh, come on now," Emma said in exasperation. "Surely you thought of that."

"No," Matt replied.

"Not even," Paul agreed.

Chaudhary came to a stop beside them. "Miss Emma does have quite the point, you know. Cutting the extremities off would lighten the load."

"Dismemberment seems kind of harsh, don't you think?" Paul asked.

"Not if it helps us maintain control of the mummy." Emma faced Matt. "Don't you dare say anything. You were the one who decapitated that body in the first place."

"It's a good idea," Matt admitted.

"We may be able to sacrifice the abdomen as well. I haven't seen anything there that we might need."

"Enough," Paul said in a hoarse voice. "I'd rather not know the details, thank you. I'd hate to be sick while we're trying to make our getaway."

The men with the lanterns kept going. After they'd disappeared, Matt waited another few minutes, then stepped outside and flagged down a cab. They quickly piled into the vehicle and gave directions to a pub on Fleet Street.

Matt's mind kept sifting through the information they'd gleaned. Even with the knowledge that they could probably trigger the mummy's image apparatus again, he still didn't know what they were looking for. They needed more. And they knew precious little about what Creighdor was working toward.

Turning to Paul as he thought about the information Gabriel had revealed, Matt said, "You've met Geoffrey Fiske, haven't you?"

"Geoffrey?" Emma lifted her eyebrows in surprise.

"You know Geoffrey?" Paul asked.

"Of course. He and his father have been at several royal parties where my father maintained security. His father is a very important man in this city. Is Geoffrey part of this?"

"That," Matt said, "is something we're going to find out."

"Do you think they'll rob us in a nice, respectable manner?" Paul asked. "Or do you suppose they'll simply gut us and be done with the job?"

Matt didn't blame Paul for having misgivings. East End was one of the worst places to be in all of London, especially at night. And the particular neighborhood they were presently in was even worse.

Tenement buildings ringed them on all sides. Hard, merciless men roved the cobblestone streets. Pubs did a raucous business. Few cabs worked the area, though no few came into it. The privileged came calling on the poor and the desperate for things they could not get in their safe and secure neighborhoods.

After paying their driver, Matt took the lead, heading for the alley to the north. Paul fell in beside him.

"How do you know this is the place?" Paul asked.

"Because Gabriel told me." Gabriel had found out only that afternoon where the backstreet gambling arena was. From what he'd told Matt, the ratter's game roved throughout the city, always managing to stay one step ahead of the metropolitan police. Paul's inquiries had garnered the information from among his friends that Geoffrey Fiske intended to go ratting that night.

"Gabriel could have been misinformed."

"If he was, then a number of others were too." Matt nodded at the half-dozen men ahead of them who wore gentlemen's clothing.

The alley led to an entrance of a basement arena that reminded Matt of the basement they'd examined the mummy in the previous night. A hulking doorman guarded the premises.

"'Ello, gentlemen," the doorman greeted in a deep voice that carried no note of true welcome. "There's a small matter of an entrance fee, there is."

Matt paid for both of them, then the doorman

opened the way. "Just follow the tunnel, gentlemen," he instructed. "You'll find the games just beyond."

The tunnel was short and filled with the noxious odors of human sweat, blood, and offal. Thunderous shouts and a gleeful frenzy sounded from just ahead. Another doorman at the end of the hallway motioned Matt and Paul on through.

Inside the large basement room, dozens of men ringed an earthen pit dug in the floor. Wooden pallets from the docks, overlaid with plywood, were nailed into a rough square around the pit. Hard-knuckled men and men in crisp suits held drinks and wads of cash. A blue-gray cloud of cigar and pipe smoke hugged the low ceiling and fought against the lanterns hanging on the walls and over the pit.

"Have you ever been to anything like this?" Paul asked.

"Once," Matt answered. "I didn't care for it." The memory of the visit almost made him sick.

"I've heard of ratting," Paul said, leaning close to be heard, "but I've never wished to see it. Turned down several invitations, in fact." He gazed around the crowd. "I've always heard this was entertainment for the poverty-stricken of London."

The mix of well-to-do and hard-pressed men ringing the pit and shouting their good fortune or their ill luck bore noisy rebuke to that.

"This is entertainment for the bloodthirsty," Matt said. "Wealth doesn't separate savages."

A fat man stepped up onto a keg in front of the pit. He wore banker's clothes and a tall hat that he had to take off in order to fit under the low ceiling.

"Gentlemen," the fat man yelled.

The crowd quieted somewhat.

"Tonight's a night of rare privilege," the fat man went on. "For tonight is the night Lord Cheswell has deemed that his ferocious terrier— the mighty fighter, Sinbad, with nearly a hundred victories to his good name—should return to grace our pit with his cunning grace and razor-sharp jaws."

An elderly man approached the pit with a manservant at his side. Both were well dressed. The manservant carried a wooden cage containing a trembling black-and-white terrier. Even from a distance Matt saw that scars criss-crossed the dog's face. One eye socket was fitted with a bright blue marble.

A cheer came from several of the men, all of whom seemed eager to bet on the dog.

Lord Cheswell frowned, obviously not pleased with the crowd of admirers who wouldn't bet against him. "It's been months since you've seen Sinbad fight. Well, we'll see how much you believe in my hound. Tonight Sinbad is going up against fifteen rats."

"Ah, Sinbad's kilt fifteen afore," a grimy man

with two missing front teeth scowled. "I ain't gonna bet against you with odds like that."

Matt looked around the room as the bidding ensued. In short order, the spectators pushed the lord into staking his dog against twenty-four rats in the pit. Lord Cheswell cursed ferociously, but he obviously wanted to gamble. Matt felt sorry for the dog.

Sinbad was lowered into the pit and released. The dog trotted nervously around the bloody earth, lowering its muzzle to sniff out previous combatants. Then cages of large sewer rats were lowered into the pit and the fight began.

Instead of running from the rats, the dog attacked at once. Several of the bettors complained that the dog's attack was premature and unfair because not all of the rats had been released from the cages. Matt knew the animal was going by its past history of fighting in the pit, crunching skulls, snapping necks, and eviscerating its opponents as quickly as possible to cut down the odds.

The yelling became even more frenzied as the dead rat bodies began to litter the bloody ground.

Matt noticed that Paul had turned ashen. His friend's grip on his walking stick threatened to snap even the steel blade hidden within. Then Paul jerked his chin forward, alerting Matt.

Turning, Matt saw Geoffrey Fiske standing at the pit railing with a wad of pound notes in his fist. Bloodlust lined his taut features. He was young and handsome, but the savage within him had definitely come out to play.

By the time Matt forced his way through the crowd to reach the young man's side, the terrier had gone down under a pile of rats. Blood matted the fur of the dog and the rats till they were inseparable. Lord Cheswell clung to the edge of the pit and screamed for someone to save his dog, while other men shouted out in glee and told the old man to pay up.

"There now!" Geoffrey shouted happily, turning to Matt in his exuberance. "I knew that dog couldn't take twenty-four rats! It was too old! Anyone could see that! That old fool let his pride lose him his dog and his money!"

"Mr. Fiske," Matt said.

Geoffrey looked at Matt, some of his ebullience fading as he obviously sensed trouble on the way. "I don't know you."

"No," Matt said in a calm, firm voice, "but I know you, Mr. Fiske. You owe a lot of people money. It would be a tragedy if your father were to find out, don't you think?"

"What do you want?" Geoffrey squinted and twitched. He put his hand to his left ear.

The gesture reminded Matt of Locke's behavior and Nigel Kirkland's before that. "The money that you owe Shank Hutchins," Matt said. Information about that debt had come through Gabriel's contacts.

"That's been paid," Geoffrey protested.

"Not according to these." Matt fanned out the promissory notes Gabriel had forged. They even carried the mark of Shank Hutchins on them. "Shank sold me your markers, Mr. Fiske. I've come to collect on my investment."

"That's wrong," Geoffrey said, looking at the notes. "Mr. Hutchins has received his pay. Mr. Creighdor paid him. I saw him do it. You've been sold these markers in bad faith."

"Maybe I should talk to Mr. Creighdor, then."

"He will only send you away," said Geoffrey. Then, without warning, the young man suffered through a painful attack of some sort that left him pale and shaking. He covered his ear.

"What's wrong with you?" Matt asked.

"Nothing. A recurring earache. I've seen my physician about it."

Matt held Geoffrey's gaze for a moment, keeping his face harsh and impassive. "What do you think Mr. Creighdor will say when he finds out you've been borrowing money from lenders he's already paid off for you?"

"Don't. Please. We can come to some kind of terms." Geoffrey fumbled inside his coat and brought out a blue bottle. Before he could open it, though, the pain slammed into him again, taking him down to his knees.

The blue bottle rolled away from Geoffrey's palsied hand.

"My pills!" Geoffrey cried. "Please! My pills! I need them!"

Paul knelt beside Geoffrey. Looking up at Matt while holding Geoffrey's shoulders, he said, "He's going into convulsions. Get the pills."

Matt bent down to pick up the blue bottle still rolling across the hardwood floor. Before he could close his fingers on it, a small gloved hand snatched the bottle from his grasp. He looked up and found he was face-to-face with Jessie Quinn.

Chapter 14

Jessie Quinn smiled in triumph as she held the blue bottle. "Lord Brockton," she greeted.

Matt stared at the young woman, his mind instantly filled with a hundred questions. "Miss Quinn, it appears we meet again."

"In the unlikeliest of places," Jessie agreed. She nodded toward the pit. "I would have never figured you for somethin' like this, though." She paused. "I thought you were more the type for polite society."

"That is my preference."

Jessie glanced at his coat. "I see you brought your pistols to town just the same."

Matt said nothing.

Looking at the blue bottle, Jessie asked, "Are you sick?" Although she was smiling, no levity touched her dark eyes.

"That's not mine," Matt said. "It's for a friend." He pointed back the way he'd come but found that at least a half-dozen men stood between Paul and Geoffrey and him.

Geoffrey yelled then, and the men standing between them stepped aside as Geoffrey pushed himself across the dirty floor with one hand held to his ear.

"I see." Jessie frowned irritably. She flipped the bottle to Matt. She wore a black dress that fit her well.

"You shouldn't be in a place like this alone," Matt said.

"I'm not alone," Jessie said. "An' even if I was?" She smiled and cocked an eyebrow. "I'd be fine enough."

Matt quickly stood and reached down to help Jessie up. He was surprised at the strength in her grip.

"These men in here have probably never shot anybody before," Jessie said, her eyes flashing as she fixed him with her stare. "Probably never killed anything bigger'n a fly. Instead, they choose to watch these poor animals fight to the death an' call it a sport. I guess seein' all that blood spilt makes 'em men in their minds."

"You are plainspoken, Miss Quinn," Matt said.

"I am. I embarrass my daddy at times. My momma, she's come to expect it. She says I was never purely raised right. Blames it on my Apache blood I get through her mother, who took off for a time with an Apache brave. Maybe my momma's right. Anyways, she forgives me when I get out of line."

Geoffrey howled in pain and pushed himself to a standing position with Paul's help. Holding his hand out, Geoffrey said, "Two! Now!"

Matt poured the pink pills into Geoffrey's outstretched hand. Chewing rapidly and grimacing, Geoffrey swallowed. Men made room for him at the pit wall, and he barely remained standing under his own power.

"How about you?" Jessie asked.

"Excuse me?" Matt replied.

The dark eyes searched his. "Have you ever killed anybody?" she asked.

Matt was taken aback. "That's hardly an appropriate question."

"I'm hardly ever appropriate."

"What are you doing here?" Matt asked.

"Seein' the sights." Jessie shrugged in a manner that was totally unladylike but on her, with her relaxed air, it fit. "Mr. Creighdor thought maybe I would enjoy this."

"Creighdor brought you here?"

"Yes."

"Why?"

"I guess because I'm from Texas an' he knows I've killed people." A small grin twisted Jessie's lips. "I think he finds that fascinatin' about me. Personally, I think his fascination is mostly amusin'. Kind of like a young pup that has hold of a bear. He's got hold of me, but he don't know what to do with me. I like keepin' a man tangled-footed. Makes things more interestin'. Don't you think?"

Matt felt uncomfortable standing as close to her as he was. "I wouldn't know," he said.

"Well, if you figure it out, you let me know."

Paul joined them. He touched his hat briefly. "Miss Quinn."

"Mr. Chadwick-Standish," she replied, turning her attention to him.

"I'd not expected to find you here," Paul said.

"Ain't hardly one of the queen's balls, now is it?" she agreed.

"No."

Looking past them, Jessie asked, "How are you boys feelin' about another hoo-raw with Mr. Creighdor about now? Or would you rather catch a breath of fresh air? 'Cause yonder he comes."

Following Jessie's line of sight, Matt spotted Creighdor and three men making their way toward them. Creighdor didn't look happy.

"I think we'll pass on that," Matt said.

"Don't blame you," Jessie said. She looked at Matt in open wonder. "What is it about you that puts such a burr up his butt?"

Matt ignored the question, though he felt his face color a little from how indelicately she'd framed it. "Thanks for your assistance, Miss Quinn."

"Sure. Maybe I'll see you around again some time. London ain't as big as Texas, you know, an' I run into people I know there all the time. Course, there's some that light a shuck ever time they see me comin'. A matter of self-preservation."

Heading around the fighting pit opposite Creighdor and his group, Matt aimed for the door. By the time he reached it, he and Paul were shoving people aside.

Outside, they ran through the alley till they reached the street. Matt caught a hansom cab just as the driver off-loaded two men in evening-wear. As he and Paul hauled themselves aboard, Matt gave the driver an address in Fleet Street where he knew he could get word to Gabriel. Then he sat at the window with the Webleys in his lap as Creighdor and his men stepped out into the alley.

Creighdor held his men up with a hand, stopping them at the alley's mouth.

Matt checked the buildings for gargoyles but found them mercifully free of the creatures.

"Fleet Street?" Paul echoed.

"We're going to pick Gabriel up," Matt said. "We're going to need him."

"Why?"

"Because we're going to burgle a doctor's office." If things had not been so serious, Matt would have laughed at the surprised look on Paul's face.

• • •

"I thought you were a good burglar," Paul complained.

Kneeling in the dark alley in front of the lock on the back door of Dr. James Dorrance's home and medical office in Southwark, Gabriel said, "I *am* a good burglar. Unfortunately, the bloody doctor's got 'isself quite the lock back 'ere, 'e 'as. No 'elpin' that. I'll 'ave it in just a bit. Or maybe you'd like a turn at 'er?" He offered his lock picks.

Paul declined and Gabriel set back to the task.

Matt stood out in the alley with his hands on his pistols as he watched over his friends. A fine mist had blown in from the sea and proceeded to fall for the last hour, drenching everything and everyone foolish enough to be out in it. Rain slid down his coat and brought a biting chill.

"Does anyone know where Dr. Dorrance is tonight?" Paul asked, glancing up at the dark windows of the flat above the medical office. "I'd rather not break in on him while he's sleeping. If he is working with Creighdor, he might well be armed."

"Catch 'im nappin'," Gabriel said, "an' maybe we get to ask 'im a few questions about them little blue bottles what 'as pink pills in 'em."

Furtive footsteps sounded in the darkness.

Gabriel stood quickly and pressed himself into the shadows of the doorway. Matt took his pistols out of his coat and hid at the corner of the building across from Gabriel. Paul unsheathed his sword and stood ready behind him.

Only a moment later, Narada and Jaijo Chaudhary entered the alley from the street. Both of them wore dark clothing.

Matt put his pistols away and stepped out so he could be seen. He greeted the father and son.

Jaijo Chaudhary was a seventeen-year-old version of his father. He was built leaner and wore round-lensed glasses. Although he'd known of his father's past dealings with Lucius Creighdor and had met Roger Hunter, Jaijo wasn't totally accepting of Matt. He had made it clear that he thought Matt was going to get them all killed.

"Lord Brockton," Narada greeted. "I got your message and came as quickly as I could."

"What are we doing here?" Jaijo demanded.

"I'm beginning to suspect that Dr. Dorrance is in league with Creighdor," Matt said. Quickly he outlined the fact that the prescription bottles Nigel Kirkland and Geoffrey Fiske had bore labels made out in Dr. Dorrance's name. "Those bottles were filled with pink pills, and both of them suffer from excruciating earaches."

"As did Edwin Locke," Narada said.

"Yes."

"You saw no such label on the bottle that Mr. Locke had?" Narada asked.

"No."

"It ain't nuffink for a bloke to peel a label off, guv," Gabriel said as he worked. "A man in Locke's line of business, why it'd be second nature for 'im to peel off anything what might be used to identify 'im should something go wrong while 'e was where 'e wasn't supposed to be."

"We're here risking our lives because those men have earaches?" Jaijo sounded as though he couldn't believe it.

Narada addressed his son in their native language. Jaijo contritely bowed his head, but his dark eyes blazed behind his round lenses.

"We're here to take a look at the good doctor's offices," Paul said. "Since none of us are versed in chemical compounds and compositions, we thought your expertise was required."

"Ah," Gabriel exclaimed, standing up. He twisted the doorknob, bowed like a proper butler, and pushed the door inward. "You see, I am a good burglar."

Twenty minutes later, the time marked by Matt's pocket watch, they had performed a cursory search of Dr. James Dorrance's medical offices. Gabriel had also ascertained that the doctor was not at home in the flat above. They'd covered the office windows with thick blankets from the doctor's personal quarters so they could work by lantern light and remain unobserved.

The outer office was small, allowing for a nurse to take information at a small table. Five patient chairs lined the wall on each side of the door to the street.

The surgery in the back was larger. Two beds occupied the floor, and a sheet that could be unfurled from the ceiling allowed privacy. A cabinet on one wall held surgical instruments and tins and jars containing medicinal salves and powders. Narada took a lantern and studied the chemicals.

Matt, Paul, and Jaijo scoured the room. Another smaller room was beyond the back door of the surgery. The door was locked.

"I'll get Gabriel," Paul offered.

"There is no need. I can open the door." Jaijo touched the hinges on the door, then took a small hammer and a rat-tail file from Dorrance's instruments. He quickly removed the hinge pins from the door and took away the door. "Simple mechanics. It is a mistake to put the hinges of a locked door on the outside of the door. Probably the physician did not know that."

"Well," Paul said, lifting his lantern and shining it into the room, "I suppose it does keep the honest folk out."

Inside the room a few short shelves filled the small space nearly to overflowing. A table against the back wall provided working space.

When he shined the lantern over the shelves, Paul cursed. The light burned through jars and large bottles, which contained preserved reptiles, fish, fowl, and mammals.

Disquiet instantly filled Matt to the brim as he took in the macabre scene. In school he'd seen preserved specimens, but there had always been something unnatural about it, though Emma had never been of that opinion. In Matt's mind, when something was dead, it was supposed to be buried and returned to the earth.

Ropes of big snakes filled large jars. In many of the containers more than one specimen was included. Others held rats, bats, cats, the head of a dog, birds, insects, and fish. The stink of formaldehyde formed an undercurrent to the other smells in the room.

"Well," Paul said, "I daresay that if Dr. Dorrance's regular clientele saw his singular collection they'd find a new physician to consult."

Matt shone his beam across the rows of dead things. "This isn't a hobby. He's conducting a study."

"If he's got a dead body tucked away in here, I'm not staying." Paul reluctantly pressed on, moving away from the jars to focus on the books lining the wall near the tiny work space.

"I think he sees himself more as a scientist than a physician," Jaijo whispered.

"So what is his field of study?" Hypnotized by the unblinking eyes of a frog bigger than his head, Matt took the jar from the shelf. In addition to the full-grown frog, other jars—like tiny Chinese boxes, each one fitting inside the other— were inside the big jar. The other containers held four other frogs in various stages of metamorphosis, beginning with a tadpole.

"Evolution seems to be a big theme," Paul commented, drawing a book down from the shelf. "Here's a copy of Darwin's book about his journey aboard the *Beagle*." He replaced the book and took down another. "And here are several on Egyptology."

"That interest ties him to Creighdor." Matt put the jar of frogs back on the shelf and went to join Paul.

"There are several people in London who are interested in Egyptology," Jaijo pointed out. "My father's store would suffer greatly were those people not to exist."

"Dorrance also has several journals among his collection of books." Paul took another book down and opened it.

Matt looked over his friend's shoulder and saw sketches of a dog laid open by a surgeon's scalpel. The drawing was of artistic caliber and done in great detail.

Paul slammed the book shut. "Now *that* I did not need to see. At any time in my life." He shuddered and started to put the book back on the shelf.

"No," Matt said, taking the book from Paul's grasp. "We take this. We take all of the physician's records of what he's been doing in this field. Perhaps one of them will give us a clue about what he's doing with Creighdor."

"This could be just the gruesome hobby of an unbalanced mind," Paul said.

"Also," Jaijo put in, "the physician will know someone has invaded his premises."

"Doesn't matter," Matt replied, moving down the line of books for the next journal. "Knowing that someone was here will make him nervous. If he is working for Creighdor, maybe what we do here tonight will extend the feeling."

"You want to warn them that we suspect they are connected?" Paul asked.

Matt shook his head. "I want to serve them notice that the game is about to change. They no longer know all the rules or hold all the cards."

"There are some books on Egyptology you should take as well, Lord Brockton," Narada said. "Some of them are very rare. I haven't even heard of three of them. Four are very hard to find. Two of them I didn't think really existed."

"That's a lot of books." Matt held his arms out as Narada burdened him. "Isn't there something we can carry them in?"

"Pillowcases," Gabriel said as he entered the room. He carried a clutch of pillowcases in one fist. "Every good thief knows pillowcases is best for carryin' off ill-gotten gain. I went ahead an' nicked 'em whilst I was upstairs. Thought you'd probably find something interestin'." He smiled. "I know I did." He started to hold up a small glass jar, then noticed all the shelves full

149

of specimens around him. "All right, then. This makes my own small discovery look piddlin'."

As Gabriel swirled the jar around, the dark thumb-sized shape inside jerked into motion. It glided effortlessly through the liquid. As small as the creature was, though, Matt got the same feeling he had while watching a shark cut through the sea.

"It's alive," he whispered in awe.

Chapter 15

L et me see that." Matt took the vial from the young thief, shifting the load of books over. He held the small jar up against the lantern so he could see the creature inside more clearly.

"It's alive?" Paul asked.

Matt shook the jar and the creature moved again. This time he saw the fluctuations of several tiny appendages. It had a squidlike appearance, but the bulbous head, if that's what it was, flared out in different directions like a chicken's foot. And its movement was still unnerving on a subconscious level he didn't understand.

"Yes. It is," Matt answered.

"Lookin' at it makes my skin crawl," Gabriel admitted.

Matt silently agreed.

"That can't be formaldehyde it's in, then." Paul approached and added his own light.

The creature inside the jar recoiled from the

light, then curled into a ball. Its appendages waggled in the liquid, maintaining its floating position equidistant from the sides of the glass container.

"Formaldehyde would kill it," Paul whispered. "Whatever it's in, Dorrance chose to keep this one alive."

"'Ad it 'id good too, 'e did." Gabriel quickly stuffed the books Matt had given him into one of the pillowcases. "'Ad 'isself a 'idey-'ole up under 'is bed what most people would 'ave missed." He smiled. "But me, I ain't most people. Took me a couple thumps across the floor to find it. Most people live alone like this, they ain't ones without their secrets." He pulled journals from his coat pockets. "Found these up there in that 'idey-'ole too. Looks like they's writ in 'is own 'and. At least, they're writ in somebody's 'and. Since 'e 'ad 'em 'id I guessed they might be important."

"Please," Narada said, reaching out a shaking hand. "Let me see the creature." His voice had taken on a dry, papery quality. "That thing could be dangerous. Very dangerous. If it's what I believe it must be."

Apprehensive because of Narada's behavior as well as his own preternatural warning and the feeling of wrongness that tugged at the pit of his stomach, Matt handed him the jar and watched as Narada gazed upon it with a rapt expression of awe and horror. "Do you know what it is?" Matt asked.

"No," Narada answered. "But I do know what it's supposed to be." He tapped the glass with a fingernail.

The creature inside unfolded, revealing the chicken-foot appendage again.

"In some of the books I have read," Narada said, "I have seen drawings of a creature like this. But never before has its existence been confirmed. This is truly a piece of forgotten history." He rolled the jar in his hands. "You are aware that the Egyptians worshipped the scarab beetle, Lord Brockton?"

"Yes." Matt had read parts of the books Narada had recommended to him. "Because the Egyptians thought the scarab had the secret of immortality."

"That's right. Well, the term they used for this thing translates literally to 'The Voice of the Gods.' According to legend, not any history I have ever read, the Outsiders used these creatures to control their enemies and personal servants."

"How?"

Narada shook his head. "I don't know. Perhaps the books Gabriel found will offer some illumination."

Metallic clicks sounded in the room.

Recognizing the sound immediately as the hammer of a revolver locking back into the firing position, Matt spun and reached for his own revolvers.

153

"Don't," a feminine voice out of the darkness warned. "You're an interestin' man, Lord Brockton. It'd be a shame to end up dead."

Paul turned his light toward the doorway, illuminating Jessie Quinn standing there with a Colt revolver in one fist. This pistol was larger than the one she'd carried at Pender Glassworks. She wore breeches, boots, a man's shirt, and a long coat. In the darkness she could have passed as a young man.

"I wouldn't get any ideas if I was you," Jessie said, her gaze taking in the others standing there. "I can pin the ears back on a movin' jackrabbit with this pistol. Shootin' five people in a small room like this wouldn't be any chore at all. Like plinkin' fish in a barrel." She paused, her eyes locked on Matt. Desperation glinted in her gaze. "I wouldn't want to do it, but I would. So if you'll just hand me that critter an' them books, I'll be on my way."

"What are you doing here?" Matt asked.

"Same as you, I reckon. I saw that little blue bottle at the rat pit. An' Dr. Dorrance's name on it. Figured I'd come callin' on Dr. Dorrance's office, see what I could see. You just beat me to it, is all." Jessie's voice hardened. "I ain't got time to dicker about this, so I'm gonna ask you one more time, then I'm gonna shoot you where you're standin'."

"Matt," Paul said quietly, "I think she means what she's saying."

"Why do you want these things?" Matt asked.

A stubborn look settled on Jessie's face. "I got reasons of my own."

"You might not be able to get all of us if you start shooting."

"You won't know," she told him coldly. "My first bullet is goin' straight through your heart. Maybe the rest of your friends will decide to throw in their hands an' sit this one out."

Matt stood still, knowing he had no choice.

Then someone shoved a key into the outer door and turned the lock. During the day the noise would have been lost, but in the night the sound echoed through the three rooms.

For a split second, Jessie's attention wavered. Or maybe she had more trouble pulling the trigger than she'd said.

Matt lunged forward, throwing himself into the young woman and knocking both of them to the floor. He wrapped his hand around her gun wrist and tried to hold her down, but she was stronger than he'd given her credit for. She also fought dirtier than he'd expected. She brought a knee up into his crotch that he was only just able to avoid. They rolled on the floor of the surgery in their struggles.

Light splintered the darkness as someone opened the front door of the receiving room. An elegantly dressed man held a lantern and stared at Matt, Jessie, and the others in astonishment. His jaw dropped but he didn't seem able to find words.

A big hand fell on the man's shoulder and yanked him back out of the doorway. Then a man stepped into the doorway holding a shotgun, immediately aiming at Jessie and Matt.

"Let go!" Jessie ordered.

Knowing she was the only one who had a chance at a shot, Matt released her gun wrist. She adjusted the pistol in the space of a heartbeat while lying upside down on the floor. The muzzle flash spat out and a basso boom filled the room.

The .44-caliber bullet caught the big man in the face and punched him back out of the door.

Before Matt could recover, Jessie had the pistol pointed at his head.

"Get off me," she ordered.

"We're on the same side," Matt protested.

"I ain't interested in takin' sides," Jessie told him. "Now move. I ain't kiddin'."

Cries for help sounded out in the alley.

Matt stood, his every move covered by Jessie Quinn's big revolver. "Do you know Dorrance?" he asked.

"Give me that critter an' those books," Jessie ordered.

"Was that Dorrance?" Matt asked.

"I ain't got time for—"

"Because if that was Dorrance and the man you killed was a bodyguard Creighdor sent with him, this isn't ov—"

A booming crash sounded at the front of the

building. Matt reached for his pistols as a gargoyle crashed through the doorway. Its wingspan was too large for the door, so the creature tore the entrance larger. Plaster and stone rained down around the gargoyle as it turned its gaze on them.

Paul, Narada, Jaijo, Gabriel, and Emma took cover.

"What is *that*?" Jessie shouted.

Matt brought up both pistols and fired. One bullet missed, taking out a chunk of the doorway, but the other tore away half of the gargoyle's face, revealing the wires beneath. It ran forward, followed immediately by others. The second doorway stopped the gargoyle again, but it started tearing through, spilling the shelves of chemicals.

Firing again and again, aiming for the thing's head, Matt pushed Jessie along with his elbow. "Run!" The others were already in motion.

Caught by surprise, Jessie stumbled and nearly fell, but she quickly caught herself and got underway.

"This way!" Gabriel yelled. "The stairs go up to the flat!"

Jessie stepped away and brought her pistol up again. She fired once and a huge hole appeared in the gargoyle's stony chest. The creature continued tearing at the doorway to the surgery.

Matt fired again, and this time the round shattered the remainder of the gargoyle's head. "You have to shoot their heads! Go!"

Jessie turned and ran, sprinting for the stairs where the others had already gone. She caught up to the lantern hanging on a hook by the stairs and swung around to throw it at the second gargoyle already thrusting aside the wreckage of the first. Her pistol barked an instant later.

The lantern jerked and went to pieces almost at the doorway when the bullet struck it. Droplets of flaming oil splattered the gargoyles and the walls. Then pools of the spilled chemicals from the shattered shelves *whooshed* and ignited in twisting blue and yellow flames.

By the time Matt reached the top of the stairs close on Jessie's heels, the surgery blazed at every corner. Heat and smoke flew up the stairwell.

The fire didn't slow the gargoyles, though. Once they cleared the door, they ran unmindful through the flames.

Gabriel led the way, hurrying into the small bedroom and through the window overlooking the street. Matt held the gargoyles at bay for a time, firing his pistols judiciously till both emptied. He turned to flee just as one of the gargoyles, already bearing damage from his marksmanship but not yet destroyed, leaped up the stairwell after him.

The thing caught his ankle in a bone-crushing grip. He turned as best as he could and hammered at the gargoyle's broken head with his pistols. He knew he couldn't escape; the damage he was able to do with the pistols wasn't enough.

Then a series of rapid-fire shots rang in Matt's ears. Six rounds, coming like rolling thunder, shattered the gargoyle's arm and then its head.

"Come on!" Jessie called. She sat in the window, coolly and methodically dumping empty shells from her weapon.

Matt pushed himself up and ran. He pushed the pain of his leg from his mind and climbed through the window. Jessie slid down the eaves ahead of him. He went over the edge and very nearly landed on her in the street. Paul gave him a hand up as Jessie rolled to her own feet.

"What are those things?" Jessie thumbed cartridges from the belt around her hips and reloaded.

Matt shook the brass from his own pistols and reloaded from the rounds he kept in his pockets. "Gargoyles."

"Look," Jessie said, earring the hammers back on her Colts, "maybe we don't have gargoyles back in Texas, but I been around enough of 'em here in England to know that gargoyles don't come alive."

Matt didn't argue. A brief glance at the building showed that it was going up in flames. He hated to see that. Fire was one of London's greatest enemies. Once set free in the city, a fire could sweep through entire neighborhoods in minutes and eradicate everything in its path.

Following Gabriel, the group ran through

the streets and alleys and empty lots, finally ending up at a crowded pub when Narada Chaudhary could no longer keep up. They spread out at once, choosing spots so they could look out doors or windows all the way around the building.

Matt made himself relax and loosen his hold on the pistols in his pockets.

"Are we safe here?" Jessie asked.

"We should be. Creighdor's gargoyles don't usually appear where a lot of people can see them." Matt kept his attention divided between the street outside and Jessie Quinn.

She stared at him. "Those gargoyles wear Creighdor's brand?"

It took a moment for her words to register. "I guess that's one way of putting it."

Jessie stared at Matt. "How much do you know about the pills in those little blue bottles?"

"Very little," Matt admitted. "So far. I didn't know they were important. Until tonight."

"Your friend at the fight pit."

Matt shook his head. "Geoffrey Fiske isn't a friend. He's part of one of Creighdor's little games."

"What have you got against Creighdor?" Jessie asked.

Matt looked at her, remembering how quick and deadly she could be. Still, England wasn't her home. She was already out of her depth. He didn't want the responsibility for involving her any further than she'd managed on her own. "No."

"I still need that critter you found. And those books."

"Why?"

Jessie paused, studying him. "Are you a man of your word, Matt Hunter?"

Matt returned her gaze full measure. "Yes."

"Then trade me."

Not understanding, he said, "Trade you what?"

"Stories. It's something we do in Texas."

"What story?"

"I'll tell you why I want those things, then you tell me what you're fightin' Creighdor for."

Matt considered the offer and decided to turn her down. Whatever secret she was holding, he would find out soon enough.

"I went there," Jessie said, as if reading his thoughts, "because I want to help my daddy. Creighdor has been workin' with him, tryin' to build up business around Texas. President Cleveland sent my daddy here to see about doin' some commerce. Balancin' imports an' exports between the States an' England."

Matt was impressed with her knowledge. "You don't often find women who talk about such things."

"Don't you underestimate me, mister," Jessie said. "I may sound like a hick to you, with all your citified ways, but I grew up on a workin' cattle ranch. That's a hard business for anybody. Profit an' loss, that's what all that business is about. Buyin' land, acquirin' grazin' an' waterin' rights. You gotta grow or dry up an' blow away in Texas. My daddy built a big ranch out there, an' we all help out. Ain't nothin' ever been give to any of us."

"All right. I won't underestimate you." And Matt promised himself he never again would.

"Since we been here, my daddy got sick. Some kind of stomach trouble. Bad enough for him to go to a doctor."

"I don't understand—"

"Creighdor recommended a doctor." Unshed tears glimmered in Jessie's eyes. "Want to guess who Creighdor recommended?"

Matt felt like the earth had just opened up beneath him. "Dorrance," he whispered.

"Right," Jessie said fiercely. "Now my daddy carries around one of them blue bottles an' he don't act like himself. I been hangin' around Creighdor tryin' to find out what's goin' on. He thinks it's because he's a handsome man. Guys with prideful ways, well, they're just big targets, is all." Her voice became strained and she swallowed hard. "Now this here's all the warnin' you get. Either you help me find out what's wrong with my daddy or I'm gonna fight you with ever' breath left in me."

Matt looked at her, knowing that she wasn't going to go away and that she meant every word she'd said. "Creighdor had my father killed," he said hoarsely. "Before that, he and a man named Josiah Scanlon were responsible for the murder of my mother." He pushed the emotion away for a moment. "There's too much to tell here. We still have to get away."

"Then you tell me where, because I'm not leaving till I get the whole story," Jessie declared. "Fair is fair."

Eyes burning and head pounding from days of getting too little sleep and staying up the whole night before, Matt sat at a table in the offices Paul had acquired for them not far from the Thames River. Groggy, he pushed himself up from the book he'd been reading and made his way across the room to the teapot.

Sunlight stabbed through the wooden blinds that covered the window. Morning had dawned little more than an hour ago. Matt felt like last night had been a week ago.

Seated in another part of the room, Paul worked on the company ledgers, getting ready to issue another round of paychecks to the employees of Hunter businesses. It seemed like the weeks flew by. But they had yet to find a clerk they could trust to manage the payroll—and not be in Creighdor's employ—or one that could handle the rapid changes Paul made on nearly a daily basis.

I don't know how he does it, Matt thought,

looking at Paul. And he wondered again how his father had managed to carry on the family business and his private war against Lucius Creighdor for seven long years.

Jaijo had gone home to be with the Chaudhary family and to open the shop, but Narada sat at another table and pored over the books they had taken from Dorrance's office. He made notes on a ledger. So far they'd only found brief mentions of "The Voice of the Gods," always written as if about a supernatural creature instead of the living thing held captive in the jar on Matt's table.

The thing hung quietly in the liquid. Occasionally it moved. And it never failed to send a cold shiver down Matt's spine. Everything about the creature seemed unnatural.

Jessie Quinn appeared indefatigable, though. She'd confessed she wasn't much of a reader, but she'd attacked Dorrance's books without hesitation. The answers, they all hoped, were somewhere between those covers.

A light rap sounded on the door. Matt drew the Webley.

Paul, closest to the door, answered it.

Emma Sharpe, looking bright and chipper, stood in the doorway. Her cheery smile vanished immediately when she saw the state everyone was in. Even more of her good humor disappeared when she spotted Jessie seated at a table.

"Emma Sharpe, may I introduce Jessie

Quinn," Matt said. The two young women nodded at one another.

"It's all right, Emma. She's a friend." Matt put the Webley away.

Despite the introduction, Jessie watched Emma. The American girl didn't put her pistol away, choosing to leave it lying in her lap as she lifted her booted feet to the table and leaned back in the chair.

Joining Matt at the tea service, Emma whispered, "What is Jessie Quinn doing here?"

"Helping."

Emma calmly poured her tea, but her disapproval was evident. "And who chose to involve her?"

"I did."

"Did you even consider the possibility that she is going to be trouble?"

"Of course."

"I thought she was with Creighdor."

"There was a reason for that." Matt put his tea down. "Come here. I want to show you something." He crossed the room, feeling Emma's reluctance to follow him.

"I took time off from my father's office this morning to help you," Emma said. "If I'd known you already had plenty of help, I'd—"

Matt picked up the jar holding the strange creature. He tapped the side of the glass. The creature sprang into action, flaring its head into the three-clawed attack position and striking out with its tentacles to propel it through the liquid.

"Oh," Emma gasped, reaching for the jar as if drawn to it. All her irritation and disapproval vanished in a heartbeat. "What is this?"

"That," Matt told her, "is just one of the things we're trying to find out this morning."

Chapter 16

The creature was placed into the ear canal," Narada Chaudhary said, walking toward Matt with an open book in his hands. "Once it was successfully inserted, the creature made its way to the victim's brain and leached into his actions and even his very thoughts. At least, according to this account." He placed the book on the table. "At that point, the Outsider that had prepared that particular 'Voice of the Gods' could take complete command of the infected person."

"Even to the point that if an Outsider commanded a person to die, he would die?" Matt asked.

"There are cases of that very thing mentioned in the books. One account mentioned that an Outsider so despised a man that he commanded the man to cut himself to pieces, starting with his fingers and toes. According to the story, the man took nearly two days to die. Edwin Locke's hasty death was a blessing by comparison."

Matt walked over to the table, joined by Paul, Jessie, and Emma.

The drawing in the book was extremely graphic, showing the insertion of the creature into a man's ear through a long glass tube. The creature in the picture resembled the one in the jar that Emma had been studying.

Jessie hugged herself as she looked at the drawing. For a moment tears glimmered in her eyes, then she firmed her resolve and stood her ground.

Matt felt sorry for her, knowing that she was thinking of her father and the possibility that one of the creatures was now affixed to his brain.

"You said 'infected,'" Paul said.

"Yes," Narada replied. "That is this author's term, not mine." He took his glasses off and cleaned them with a handkerchief. "Personally, after reading these accounts, I would lean more toward calling a person with such a creature embedded in his head *possessed*."

"You said the Outsider that had prepared a particular creature could command the person with it in his or her head," Matt said.

Narada nodded. "These texts nearly all bear that supposition out. Two say that the creatures made the . . . afflicted persons responsive to commands from any Outsider."

"What was the purpose of the creatures?" Matt asked.

"Subjugation of the people infected," Narada answered. "Pure and simple. Horrifying, yes, but from the reports in this book, the process was one hundred percent effective. The Outsiders took over the minds of pharaohs or their advisers, merchants, and took a few men to be their bodyguards." He paused and pursed his lips in a frown. "There are other stories about terrible things the Outsiders did with the people they possessed, but I see no need to go into that."

"What about the pills?" Jessie asked.

"There is no mention of pills in the books that I have read. But there is mention of a substance the Outsiders gave to the people they inflicted with the creatures. In fact, when the Greeks later arrived and discovered the stories of the Outsiders, they named remnants of the substance ambrosia."

"'The food of the gods,'" Jessie said.

Showing obvious surprise, Emma looked at Jessie.

"Maybe I don't know everything you know an' I don't talk good as you do," Jessie said coolly, "but I been to school, an' my daddy an' momma were always entertainin' educated men at our ranch. I listened, an' I read a book ever' now an' again."

"In between gunfights and killings, no doubt," Emma said.

Rather than cursing or even threatening to take the encounter to a physical level as Matt expected and feared, Jessie smiled sweetly. "I kept myself busy."

Matt didn't know what the friction was between the two women, but it grated on his nerves. However, he'd learned enough to stay out of it, until it truly became a problem. He hoped the situation would sort itself out.

"Why were the afflicted people given the substance?" Paul asked.

"I can only guess at this point," Narada answered, "but I would have to suspect that the mixture was designed to facilitate the relationship between the creatures and their hosts."

"So the pills are an updated version of that ambrosia?" Paul asked.

"That is, at present, the answer that would seem to fit," Narada said.

"If Creighdor already had these creatures, why did he need Dr. Dorrance?" Matt asked. Although Gabriel had been out and about all morning in search of the physician, James Dorrance remained missing. Matt thought the physician's body would soon turn up in the river or a convenient sewer.

"Dorrance was the chosen vehicle of delivery," Paul said. "Creighdor has obviously recommended the doctor to the people he's been doing business with. Mr. Pender had the pills. As did

Locke, Nigel, and Geoffrey. And Miss Quinn's father, of course."

"Wait," Emma said. "If Creighdor gave Dr. Dorrance access to the creatures, why did Dr. Dorrance have one hidden under his bed?"

"That's only one of several questions we'll have to find answers to," Paul said. "If that thing is out there, we have no way of guessing how many more exist. Can you imagine what Creighdor would be able to accomplish if he succeeded in having those things implanted in a number of key people responsible for the guidance and safety of England?"

The thought left them all speechless for a moment.

"There is something you have overlooked," Emma said.

Matt looked at her and saw the knitted brows that always told him Emma was focused on a line of thought. "What?"

"You said Edwin Locke was under the command of one of those creatures. But what happened to the creature? Did you see any sign of it that night?"

Matt looked at Paul. Both shook their heads.

"Well," Emma said, "it may yet be that the creature is within Edwin Locke. If it is, I should like very much to look at it. We need to get as much information about these things as we can."

"Edwin Locke was buried in a pauper's grave days ago," Paul said.

"Do you know where?"

"No."

"Then I suggest you find out."

"Whatever for?"

"We need to dig up his body, of course. If the creature is still within Edwin Locke's head, we might be able to recover it."

Even Jessie seemed surprised at Emma's cold-blooded suggestion.

"Emma," Paul said in a dry voice. "You do realize that there is every reason to believe the creature is dead, don't you?"

"Of course I do. But even dead things have ways of giving up their secrets, Paul. That's what science is about. That's why medical schools buy corpses for their students to work on, and why the government chooses to turn a blind eye toward the practice of body snatching on occasion." Emma paused. "We need to know more about what we're facing. We also need another creature. If there's one to be had. We don't want to lose or damage the one we have to study. Bring me that body. If the creature still lies within the dead man, I shall excise it and continue our investigations. Our only other choice is to remain in the dark about Creighdor's plans."

"You want shovels an' a cart for *what*?" Gabriel wrapped his arms around himself and looked thoroughly put out.

Paul began, "So that we can exhume—"

Gabriel held up a hand and shook his head. Despite the fact that they stood in the alley outside a pub Gabriel frequented, he glanced around self-consciously. "I 'eard what it was you said. Ain't nuffink wrong with my 'earin'."

"Then what's the problem?" Matt asked.

"You're talkin' about exhumin' a man's corpse," Gabriel said. "That's the bloody problem."

"You have sold corpses to the medical colleges on occasion," Paul pointed out. "You've said so yourself."

"But I didn't dig 'em up, now did I?" Gabriel fired back. "I found them bodies in alleys an' the sewers. Wasn't nobody gonna need 'em no more."

"I'm quite sure Edwin Locke doesn't need his body any more either," Matt said.

"It ain't that," Gabriel said. "I didn't respect the man whilst 'e was still among the livin'. But with 'im dead like that—"

"Like what?" Paul challenged.

"Buried proper."

"In a pauper's grave?"

Gabriel glowered at Paul. "With church words said over 'im an' all. Diggin' 'im up after such as that just don't seem right."

"What's the difference between finding a dead man in an alley and finding one at the bottom of a grave?" Paul demanded.

"You just shouldn't go disturbin' a man's

final rest, is all," Gabriel replied. "They's laws against it."

"You seem to pick and choose between laws quite easily when you've a mind to."

"You disturb a dead man's final restin' place, you may 'ave 'is ghost on your 'eels the rest of your life. Which prolly won't be very long."

Paul laughed in surprise. "You're afraid."

A dark flush singed Gabriel's cheeks. He balled his hands into fists. "You just don't know ever'thin' that's out there in the world, Mr. 'Igh an' Mighty!"

"Ghosts aren't real."

"An' there would be some that would say that thing you go on about bein' in Edwin Locke's 'ead ain't real neither, now ain't there?"

"Stop," Matt said.

Paul and Gabriel looked at him, both on the verge of letting anger get the better of them.

"You're tired," Matt said. "All of us have been up all night, and it doesn't look like we're going to get sleep anytime soon. Not if we're going to try to figure this thing out." He took a deep breath. "Gabriel, I need those shovels, a cart, and whatever else you think it will take to get Edwin Locke's corpse. I'll go by myself if I have to. And if necessary, I'll buy shovels and a cart."

"An' if you 'ave to make a fast getaway, you might 'ave to leave them tools an' the cart behind," Gabriel said. "You'll give them bobbies an' inspectors a fair chance at catchin' you, you will."

"Either way," Matt said. "I've got to do it. I'll dig his body up with my bare hands if I have to."

Gabriel sighed grudgingly. "You'll be better off if I 'ave a few of the lads nick them tools an' cart for you round dark."

"That's why I came to you."

"I'll see that it's done for you."

"Thank you. I can dig the body up myself. There's no need for you to be there."

Gabriel nodded.

"You won't be alone, Matt." Paul grimaced and pulled on his gloves. "I'd hardly let you go traipsing round a cemetery in the dead of night by yourself. You can count on me. I'm not worried about disturbing Edwin Locke's final slumber. Nor am I concerned about ghosts."

"Thank you, Paul," Matt said quickly before the argument between his friends could begin again. "Gabriel, have you had any luck finding Dorrance?"

"None. I think 'e's left the city."

"Where would he go?"

"I don't know. I've been askin' around. Seems the doctor 'ad a 'abit of goin' out of the city on a regular basis."

"Where?"

"'Aven't found out yet. But listen 'ere. I'm still askin' round. Dr. Dorrance, 'e 'ad a cleanin' lady an' a receptionist. The receptionist is missin', like the doctor, an' the cleanin' lady 'anged 'erself last night."

"She hanged herself?" Paul repeated. "What on earth for?"

Gabriel narrowed his eyes. "Well, now, no one knows the answer to that particular question. She was a lady livin' with a few other women 'er age. 'Ad no enemies that anyone knew of. No particular sadness in 'er life."

"She was killed by Creighdor's people." The guilt returned to Matt. If he hadn't gone there, the woman might still be alive.

"It wasn't you what killed 'er, Matt," Gabriel said gently. "Was them what we're after. They might 'ave done for her even 'ad we not gone there. They wasn't 'bout to leave no trail for anyone else."

Outside, Matt peered down the street, looking for a cab.

A newsboy walked by, waving his papers in the air. "Murder! Murder! Read all about the murder!" the boy crowed. "Mortimer Fiske, engineerin' baron, murdered by the son of an English Lord! Murder! Murder! Nigel Kirkland, son of Lord Pawlton, murders Mortimer Fiske!"

"Boy," Matt called, reaching into his pocket for coins. "Two papers." He couldn't believe what he'd just heard: Geoffrey Fiske's father, dead!

The boy trotted over and exchanged two

papers for payment, then went off down the street, yelling louder because selling a murder story was obviously going to be worthwhile.

Paul flagged a cab. Matt boarded with him, giving him one of the papers. They both sat and read.

The story was brief and to the point, though the writer did try to paint pictures with colorful words and nicely turned phrases. At eight o'clock that morning, Nigel Kirkland interrupted Mortimer Fiske's breakfast and emptied a pistol into the engineering baron, killing Fiske on the spot.

Witnesses claimed that Kirkland, while showing no emotion at all during the shooting, threw himself down in an apparent fit of instant remorse. At one point Kirkland had turned the weapon on himself and tried to shoot himself in the head before police took him into custody. The young man was currently being held at the City of London police station while an investigation was performed.

Details to follow, the paper promised.

But Matt knew the reporters would never discover who was behind the murder.

"Well," Paul said as they both looked up from their papers, "I think we know where we'll be spending the next few hours." He rapped his walking stick on the top of the cab and directed the driver to take them to the police station where Nigel Kirkland was being held.

Chapter 17

Matt and Paul sat in a small dingy office inside the City of London police station while inspectors questioned Nigel Kirkland for hours. The wait seemed intolerable to Matt, but there was nothing to be done about it. Being an English lord granted a man several rights and privileges that most men didn't enjoy. But at times, even those rights and privileges came with a waiting period. Knowing what Nigel had to say was important. Until he found out whether he'd be allowed to speak with Nigel, he felt he had to stay.

Or, at least, until night came and they had to go to the graveyard to dig up the body of Edwin Locke.

Standing in the doorway overlooking the hall, Matt listened attentively as newspaper reporters jockeyed fiercely with uniformed policemen as well as inspectors in plainclothes for information about the murder. None of the journalists or inspectors had turned up a motive for the shooting. Nothing was forthcoming, but the rumor was that despite all the hours the inspectors went at Nigel, he hadn't talked. Not one word. Matt couldn't help thinking about the tentacled thing possibly adhered tightly to Nigel's brain.

"Do you think he's brain-dead then?" Matt sat on the window ledge looking out at the sun slowly dropping into the western sky. It was low enough already that it caught red and purple color in the smoke that poured from the chimney stacks of the manufacturing plants.

"Possibly."

"We could be wasting our time here."

"Do you think we should go?"

Matt sighed and turned from the door. "No. If we can, we need to find out what he has to say. Or if we can do anything to help him."

"We didn't put him here."

After a brief hesitation, Matt said, "I can't help feeling he's in the situation he's in because of us. Perhaps if we hadn't gone after him that night, he might not be here now."

"No." Paul's answer was uncompromising. "Nigel had already made his deal with the devil before we came calling a few nights ago."

Still, Matt couldn't divorce himself from the guilt that weighed on him.

"There's nothing to be done for Nigel in any case," Paul said quietly. "More than likely he will hang. Or, if his father should not want to bear the ignominy of his only son being publicly executed, Nigel might be put into an institution for the criminally insane and kept there the rest of his natural life."

And either of those endings could be my own, Matt thought.

"Lord Brockton?"

Matt turned to face the man in the doorway. "Yes."

"I'm Inspector Dawkins, your lordship." The man stood almost six feet tall. He was in his middle years, slim and fit. Gray streaked his whiskers and temples, showing against the brown hair. His suit was well kept but showing age. His demeanor was forced but not abrasive. He'd been told to report to the waiting lord, but he hadn't been happy about it. "I understand you've been waiting to speak to Mr. Nigel Kirkland."

"Yes."

"Might I inquire why you wish to see Mr. Kirkland?" Dawkins's quick gray eyes flicked from Matt to Paul and back again.

"Mr. Kirkland is Mr. Chadwick-Standish's friend," Matt said. He leaned on the social gulf that separated the lords from the commoners. During his younger years he hadn't been so inclined, but lately Paul had taught him to use the difference as a weapon by enforcing it, or as a gift by bringing someone up to that level. "Mr.

Chadwick-Standish is my friend. I came with Paul because he's concerned about his friend. I am concerned about my own friend. I should think that's simple enough, Inspector."

Dawkins shifted his attention to Paul. "Yes, well, it's perhaps a little late to be concerned about your friend, Mr. Chadwick-Standish. As I'm sure you've been told, Mr. Kirkland shot and killed Mr. Mortimer Fiske this very morning. There were several witnesses to the event."

"I've been told that several times. I've also been told that Nigel seemed under undue stress."

The inspector let the statement hang. Paul returned the favor. Since working with Paul on business ventures and the confrontations with Creighdor, Matt had learned the value of silence. Usually guilty men could not keep quiet. Or, as Paul had so often shown Matt, men wishing to make a deal could not keep quiet. At least, the less experienced of them couldn't.

"I was informed that you and Mr. Kirkland weren't close friends," Dawkins said.

Paul stood. He kept his gaze leveled like a rifle on the inspector. "Inspector Dawkins, I am not going to sit here and be subject to an interrogation by you like I am some common criminal. Nor will I suffer foolish inquiries about the measure of my friendship to a man facing his darkest hour. I honor friendships in the best way I know how, and I'll not be confronted on that issue again, sir, or I will only talk to your superiors."

Dawkins's lips pressed into a tight, hard line.

"You know who my father is," Paul continued, "and you know that he is looked upon with favor by the Queen herself. Do not tempt me to invoke his wrath, Inspector. I am here to see a friend, following my own feelings of honor and conduct. If I may not see Mr. Kirkland, do me the courtesy of letting me know so that I don't waste Lord Brockton's time sitting here for hours longer in a vain battle against the clock."

A tic flared under the inspector's right eye. He forced a smile. "No, Mr. Chadwick-Standish, I wasn't saying that. Fact is, Mr. Kirkland was told that you and Lord Brockton were here waiting, and he asked to see you. The both of you. Those are the first words he's spoken since he was brought here."

Matt was surprised, and the feeling quickly gave way to apprehension. Nigel couldn't have been expecting them to come. So why was he willing to see them?

Nigel Kirkland sat at a table in a small windowless room. He looked ill and slack in wrinkled clothing that held dark stains. Drool dripped from the corner of his mouth and blood trickled from his left ear. Bruises colored his face. Shackles bound his wrists and ankles.

Paul turned on Dawkins. "He needs a physician."

Dawkins stared back at Paul with flat eyes. "A physician's been to see him. Said he was all right enough for questioning and to be locked up."

For a murderer.

Although Matt didn't hear those words come from the inspector's mouth, he knew the man had thought them. Usually the London police had to handle a lord or a lord's son with kid gloves, even if he was guilty. Evidently the murder of someone like Mortimer Fiske, a wealthy man who had earned the favor of the Queen, changed those rules. But the fact that Nigel's father, Lord Pawlton, hadn't shown up also spoke volumes.

"Who was the physician?" Matt asked.

Dawkins looked at Matt. "Weatherly. Dr. George Weatherly."

"Out," Nigel said in a weak voice. "Out, Inspector." He swallowed. "I'll talk to my friends alone."

If he'd been a common criminal, Nigel's request wouldn't have been honored. But Dawkins was facing the scions of three families of nobility, one of them a full lord and in possession of a seat in the House of Lords. Restraining himself, the inspector nodded, left the room, and pulled the door closed behind him.

"So you come," Nigel said in weary fascination as he looked up at them. "I didn't think you would, but he said you would. He said you all had unfinished business."

"Who said we would come?" Paul asked.

Nigel licked his lips. "You know who. He told me you would come and that I should see you. And he told me I couldn't say his name." Tears ran down his face. "I can't. I've tried and I've tried. I want to tell those inspectors who made me do that awful thing." He shook his head. "The blood kept pouring out of Mr. Fiske, and he pleaded for his life. But I couldn't stop shooting. Not till the pistol was emptied." He started crying, sounding almost too weak and too beaten to continue.

"Killing Fiske was not your idea?" Paul asked.

"No! Of course not! I didn't even know the man!"

Paul waited for Nigel to calm down again.

"I was told to kill him," Nigel whispered hoarsely. "I didn't have a choice, Paul. No choice at all. I have to obey . . . him. No matter what he tells me to do. The physician put something in my ear the last time I went to him. It makes me obey him or it hurts me in the most frightful way."

"The physician? Dorrance, you mean?"

"I can't say his name either." Nigel opened his mouth, strained, but nothing came out. "But that man . . . the one who told me to give you the message . . . he made me go. Otherwise he wasn't going to pay my creditors off."

"Was Dorrance your physician?"

"No. Dr. George Weatherly is my physician.

Always has been. I was told to go to . . . the other." Nigel wiped his eyes on his shoulder. "I didn't know he was going to do that to me. I wasn't told about that—that—*thing*."

Nausea gripped Matt's stomach as he remembered the creature in the jar.

"What thing?" Paul asked.

Nigel cried some more, then beat his head against the table.

"What did Dorrance put in your ear?" Paul asked.

"It *hurts*, Paul! I can feel it inside my head! It hurts and they won't give me my medicine!" Nigel gasped and gagged and cried more. "I've had a headache for hours that's made my skull feel near to bursting! It wriggles and moves around! Like some great dog that can't quite get comfortable!"

"That's impossible," Paul said. "You can't feel it moving. The human brain is incapable of feeling."

Matt remembered Emma stating that when she'd examined the mummy's head and commented on the apparatus inside the skull. She'd reiterated that fact while talking about the creature Gabriel had found.

"Is it *your* bloody head?" Nigel shouted, throwing himself up from his chair only to fail and fall back into it. "Have you got one of these things inside your head?"

"No," Paul said, remaining calm.

185

Nigel cursed vehemently. "Then don't be bloody telling me what I can feel and what I can't! I *can* feel this!"

Paul waited a moment until Nigel had quieted down somewhat. Matt didn't think Nigel calm so much as wearied even of crying.

"We're trying to find Dr. Dorrance," Paul said. "If we do, perhaps we can find a way to help you."

"You can't help me!" Nigel exploded. "I'm going to hang for murder! That's how . . . he wanted it! I'm nothing to . . . him! Just a means to an end! He just used me to kill Mr. Fiske!" He suddenly jerked his head to one side and fell forward onto the table. For a moment he didn't breathe.

Matt reached for the door, intending to call in whoever might be eavesdropping on the other side. Then he saw Nigel's chest start moving again.

Weak and shaking, Nigel dragged his head over and looked at Paul. Bright crimson blood trickled from Nigel's ear and puddled on the table.

"It's going to kill me, Paul," Nigel whimpered. "It's going to kill me. He said it would. It'll just keep eating away at me till there's nothing left." His face crumpled and he cried. "I don't want to die. I've done bad things, but I've never done anything to deserve this. I can't even tell the police about this thing in my head. And they wouldn't believe me anyway. I had other physicians, Dr. Weatherly included, check for it, but they couldn't find anything. They said I was imagining things." His voice broke and tightened so that he was almost shrieking. "But I'm not! I swear to you, Paul, I am not imagining this!"

"I know, Nigel." Paul tentatively reached out to touch Nigel's shoulder.

Matt didn't think he'd have had the nerve to show that kind of support. What if the creature inside Nigel's head could move around? Could it attack Paul?

Silence weighed heavily in the room.

"He wanted you to know," Nigel gasped, "that this was what you had to look forward to. You and Lord Brockton. That's why he allowed me to talk to you. He said to tell you he'd have you in his thrall. You and anyone who helped you." He wheezed, breathing with effort. "He wanted you to know that. Now you need to go away. I can't talk to you anymore. I can't talk to anyone anymore."

Then Nigel's eyes closed and he lay still.

Matt's throat tightened. "Is he—"

Paul shook his head. "He's alive. Just sleeping."

At that moment, a knock sounded on the door. Matt opened it and found Inspector Dawkins standing there.

"Well then, your lordship," Dawkins said to

Matt, "you've talked with Mr. Kirkland. I think you've had enough time for that." Gazing past Matt, a concerned look fitted itself to the inspector's face.

"He's asleep," Paul said. He stood with some reluctance, and Matt knew some of the guilt that he felt. After today, probably neither of them would see Nigel again.

"Is there anything you'd like to tell me?" Dawkins asked.

"No," Paul answered.

"I see." Dawkins was grim and inflexible. He stood with his arms behind his back. "Then I'll wish you gentlemen a good evening. I have to return to my work."

Turning, Matt followed Paul through the door.

"Oh, your lordship," Dawkins called.

Matt paused and looked back at the man.

"I'd like to mention one other thing," Dawkins said. "As respectfully as I can, seeing as how you're of important station and all. Should I find that you've been anything less than truthful with me, I'll do whatever it takes to get answers from you."

"If you do proceed on that course, Inspector," Matt said, "you may not like the answers you get." He turned and left the room, following Paul out of the building. The sun was surely down by now.

They had a grave to rob.

• • •

A crimson moon peered occasionally through the black clouds that passed over the pauper's cemetery in the East End. A workhouse blocked the south end of the graveyard, while a railway line to the north, and masonry walls to the east and west that had long ago seen their best days, framed the rest of the desolate area. Mostly the poor were buried there, serviced by quick, tidy funerals and a handful of friends. They were buried just deep enough, and in wooden coffins that quickly rotted and gave up the bodies to the earth.

Some of the gravesites were well cared for, but most were overgrown, neglected. The only paths worn in the weeds and bushes that threatened to reclaim the burial grounds were from gravediggers and the church officials who saw to the burials.

Edwin Locke's grave was fresh and clean, a rectangle of broken soil in the tall grass.

In addition to getting the tools and the small wagon that sat waiting on the other side of the eastern masonry wall, Gabriel had also ascertained the gravesite, cracking jokes about not wanting to dig up the wrong dead man, that it would be even worse to have the ghost of a man they didn't know haunting them and rattling its chains.

Dressed in dark clothes, Matt dug steadily in the hole they'd started only moments ago. With the earth freshly turned, the digging was easy. Thinking about what they worked to uncover was not.

The *chuff* of the shovel biting into the earth seemed to echo over the graveyard. The wind stirred the leaves of the trees and blew a chill through Matt, cooling the layer of sweat that covered him and made his shirt stick to his flesh. He piled the earth on either side of the grave, steadily digging his way down.

In the darkness, working without a lantern and only by the intermittent moonlight, it was easy to imagine that he was digging down into an open maw that would swallow him at any moment. He tried to keep that image from his mind, but it wouldn't stay away.

"Do you need me to dig for a while?" Paul asked. He sat hunkered down by the big oak tree, staying in the shadows and watching for gargoyles. So far they hadn't seen any.

"No." Matt dumped another load of dirt. "I'm good for a few more minutes. We should be there at any time." He wore gloves to protect his hands against the rough shovel handle. Having gone over twenty-four hours without sleep, he was tired and he knew Paul was as well.

He plunged the shovel back into the dark earth. This time there was a hollow thump. Excitement and anxiety burned through him. He thrust the shovel back into the dirt and hit the solidness again.

"We've reached it," Paul whispered, and he didn't sound overjoyed at the prospect. He grabbed his shovel and clambered down into the hole.

Chapter 18

I n a few minutes Matt and Paul had cleared the wooden coffin of dirt, except for traces they couldn't remove with the shovels. Perspiration covered Matt and soaked his clothes as they stepped off the coffin and into the hole they'd dug beside it.

Hunkered down in the grave, leaning halfway over the coffin because there was precious little room to stand, Matt hooked a carpenter's hammer under the top of the coffin and yanked. Nails shrilled as they pulled free. Paul worked from the other end with a crowbar.

Struggling to get the last few nails out, Matt noticed that Paul had his knee braced on top of the coffin, making the task more difficult, though not impossible. "You've got your leg on top of the coffin."

Paul nodded. "Just to make certain that if

there's anything unpleasant inside, it won't have the chance to take us unawares."

Matt finished pulling out the last few nails. The wind picked up and the branches of the tree overhead jerked back and forth, causing strange shadows to shift across the coffin and the branches to clack like teeth gnashing.

"All right," Matt said, taking hold of the coffin top and trying not to let his imagination run rampant on him.

Paul stepped back and reached up for his walking stick. Steel rasped as he freed the blade hidden inside the ornate case. Hesitantly, he stood his ground.

Matt lifted the wooden cover and peered inside. The stink of death made his stomach roll. He forced himself to go on.

The shadows remained too thick to see the dead man's face. Then the moon came out from hiding again and trailed a brief splash of light across the pale, swollen features. Evidently the damage Edwin Locke had suffered before his strange death hadn't gone away. He'd carried his injuries to the grave with him.

"It's him," Matt declared. He reached up for the sail canvas they'd brought to wrap the body in so they wouldn't have to carry the coffin.

The two young men hauled the corpse unceremoniously from the coffin, tossed it into the middle of the sail canvas beside the grave, and then clambered up and wrapped the body with ropes. *Partly to secure the body,* Matt admitted to himself, *but partly to make certain it doesn't have a chance of moving around.*

Taking hold of the ropes binding the sailcloth, Matt and Paul carried the corpse from the grave-yard, after quickly shoveling the earth back over the grave. Lifting the gruesome burden over the cracked masonry wall where the small wagon was parked proved difficult, but they managed. They laid the mortal remains of Edwin Locke amid a small shipment of printer's supplies, then covered the body over with boxes to disguise its shape.

Matt climbed up the front of the wagon and picked up the reins. Paul settled in beside him, drawing his coat close against the night's chill.

"Do you think it's still there?" Paul asked. "The thing that was put into his head?"

Matt shook out the reins and got the horse moving. The crack of horseshoes against the cob-blestones echoed along the open railway area. "I don't know," he said.

"It could have crawled off, you know. It could have ended up anywhere."

"I know." Matt didn't know whether to wish the thing was gone or hope that it was still there inside the dead man.

Emma adjusted the lanterns around the table she was using as a surgery in back of a small aban-doned brewery. Like the time before, mirrors helped maintain the brightness on all sides. She wore a butcher's smock, which Gabriel had managed to get for her. Unfortunately, the smock—although clean—still held a collection of old and faded bloodstains. The smell of hops and barley clung to the wooden walls. The smells warred with the death odor from the corpse.

Narada worked to help Emma, arranging the scalpels and pliers. He'd offered to assist with the exploration on the man's head, but Emma had declined, insisting that she see to the job personally. If the creature was not still inside Edwin Locke's head, Emma maintained that the damage from the creature's nesting in its host's brain might tell them something.

Jessie Quinn, dressed in denim jeans, a shirt, boots, and a long, fringed rawhide jacket stood to one side. She had declined the offer of a scented handkerchief. She also wore pistols on her hips. If she was tired from staying up all night, she didn't show it. She looked deadly and focused.

Watching Emma pull on surgery gloves and reach for one of the scalpels Narada had placed at hand for her, Matt wondered again at how much he hadn't known about her. "You act like you've done this before," he said.

"I have." Emma placed the tip of the scalpel on the body's left eyebrow and circumscribed the head, slicing neatly to the bone. There was no blood.

Matt's throat suddenly felt dry. He thought for a moment he was going to be sick. Surprise at her answer distracted him, though.

"When?" Jessie asked, and there was a note of challenge in her voice, as if she didn't believe the claim. If she felt revulsion at the scene, she didn't show it.

"I am fortunate to have made the acquaintance of a young physician at the University of London." Emma put the scalpel down and slid her fingers under the edge of the flesh. "He, upon occasion, receives corpses for his students to explore and experiment on. After hours, of course, because such a study isn't humane, according to popular thinking. Though how a surgeon or scientist is supposed to learn any other way is beyond me."

Emma pulled the dead man's scalp away and dropped it into a bucket near the table.

Paul turned away and didn't watch any further.

"I was able," Emma said as she took up a pedal-powered bone saw that Narada manned, "to convince him to let me do a bit of poking around on my own." The bone saw's teeth bit into the clean white ivory of Edwin Locke's skull. More slowly this time, working the saw carefully, she inscribed the same circle around the dead man's head.

She laid the saw aside, one hand cupping the top of his skull. Easing a scalpel into the incision she'd made with the saw, she prized the skull cap off.

Despite the nightmarish sight of Emma slicing into a dead man's head, Matt's attention was transfixed on the action taking place. Holding the skull cap in her hands, Emma eased back.

At first, Matt believed the black mass that occupied the corpse's skull was Edwin Locke's brain. He thought that death had turned his brain that color. Then he saw that the mass pulsed like a heartbeat.

"Oh, my," Emma gasped.

The black mass leaped at Emma, evacuating the empty skull of the dead man with a sucking noise that echoed throughout the room. Emma screamed and raised her arms to protect her face as the creature flew toward her.

Matt was in motion at once, but Jesse Quinn was there before him. The American threw out an arm and swept Emma away as if the action were something she did every day. Her other hand had already drawn one of the .44 revolvers from her belt.

The creature flared in midair, its bulbous head splitting into the three-pronged claw that resembled a chicken's foot. The tentacles at its posterior end were no longer short and weak. Now they were thick and strong and stretched at least three feet long. The tentacles whipped forward toward Jessie's face, sliding around the bulbous mass and joining the three-toed claw in the blink of an eye. Matt had never seen anything move so quickly.

Jessie dodged, throwing herself in the opposite direction from where she'd flung Emma. She rolled and scrambled, coming up against the wall behind her.

The creature landed with a meaty splat against the stone floor, then heaved itself up again, lunging for Jessie. Since it had no apparent eyes, Matt didn't know how the thing sensed where she was. She had her pistol up, but Matt saw too late that he was in her line of fire. For a moment he thought she might fire anyway.

Paul stepped into view, letting his sword lead and his body follow. The keen blade sliced the creature in half from anterior to posterior in a horizontal stroke that missed Jessie's throat by inches. Green ichor sprayed the wall behind the creature from the force of the blow.

No longer coordinated, the two halves of the thing plopped to the floor. The tentacles moved restlessly, like broken-backed snakes, but they had no definite purpose.

Stepping in front of Jessie, his sword cane at the ready and his face and front dappled with the green fluid, Paul reached back and offered his hand. Jessie came to her feet with his help, but her pistol never wavered from the two halves of the creature on the floor.

Jessie cursed fluently. If Matt hadn't been

pumped full of fear, he might have been embarrassed.

"What is that thing?" Jessie asked when she calmed down.

"Another creature like the one Gabriel found in Dr. Dorrance's rooms," Emma said.

Matt helped Emma to her feet, feeling her shake. Her face was pale, but she didn't act afraid.

"But that thing is so much bigger than the one in the jar," Paul protested.

"It grew inside Locke's head," Emma said. "It fed on the brain or the blood. That has to be the answer."

"Do they kill the host?" Jessie looked sick. Matt knew she was thinking of her own father.

"Eventually, perhaps." Emma adjusted the lantern and shined the beam inside Edwin Locke's empty skull.

Nothing remained of the brain. The flesh inside the skull cap looked like it had been scrubbed clean. The bone gleamed like polished stone.

"This creature—" Emma sighed. "It simply must have a name. I cannot go on referring to it in this manner. I have to document my findings."

"Then give it a name, miss," Narada suggested.

Emma thought for only a moment. "Brain parasite. I think that will do."

"'Brain cannibal' would be my suggestion," Paul said.

Ignoring Paul's comment, Emma shined the lantern into the hollows of Edwin Locke's head. "As you can see, this one ate through the dead man's soft palate, devoured his tongue, and was going on through the rest of the body. Even the skull has lost several layers of bone. I suppose the brain parasite was growing, gaining strength, and harboring its resources so that it could break free of the host body. In time, perhaps, it might have gotten strong enough to dig free of the grave. It appears extremely capable of moving about on its own."

Holding his handkerchief to his mouth, Paul said, "There's not room enough in that man's head for that bloody beast."

"You mean its tentacles?" Emma handed Matt the lantern. She put a hand behind the dead man's neck and tilted his head. "If you look closely, you can see that the brain parasite had already begun its journey down into Locke's body. Probably heading for his heart, lungs, and liver first. Perhaps the stomach."

Although he didn't want to, already certain he'd have nightmares for weeks, Matt peered down into Locke's neck. Lesions on the flesh showed where the creature had already begun eating through.

"I suspect that the brain parasite would have eventually gotten strong enough to rip through the host's throat or stomach. Any of the soft tissue areas." Emma placed the head back on the table.

"Cuttin' open everybody's head that has one of them things suckin' on his brain ain't an answer I can live with," Jessie said. "My father is one of Creighdor's victims. I aim to see him free of that thing. Not dead from it." Her dark eyes sparkled with unshed tears.

"There's no guarantee that even a skillfully trained surgeon could remove the brain parasite without harming the host," Emma said. "One slip of the scalpel could reduce a patient to an idiot. Or kill him or her. The spine is that fragile."

"Has Gabriel had success in finding the physician?" Narada asked.

"Yes I 'ave," Gabriel's voice sang out. "But only just."

Chapter 19

Matt turned and found Gabriel leaning in the doorway, grinning smugly. "How long have you been standing there?"

"Just arrived, guv'nor." Gabriel crossed over to the dead man. "Ah, now 'e's certainly seen better days, 'asn't 'e?"

"Careful," Paul admonished. "You may attract his ghost. Rattling chains will keep you up all night."

Gabriel stopped, eyes fixed on the brain parasite. "An' what in bloody 'ell is that?"

"That's the big brother to the little thing you found in Dorrance's offices," Paul answered. "It got hungry while in the grave and ate Locke's brain."

"Well, it was prolly still starvin' before you up an' chopped it up, then wasn't it? If it was 'is brain it was feedin' on, why it only got a nibble from Mr. Edwin Locke, didn't it?"

"It was working on other parts. Before we interrupted its ghoulish repast."

"Gabriel," Matt said, not wanting the two to get into their usual banter. "You said you found Dorrance?"

"Well," Gabriel said, stepping around the hideous green smear the dead brain parasite had left on the floor, "I found a woman what 'elped out with the shoppin' now an' again. But she wasn't exactly forthcomin' about what she knew." He flashed a crooked grin. "Cost you a few bob for the answers, it did, but it was money well spent. She knew 'er friend didn't 'ang 'erself. Suspected foul play right off, she did. Chose to lose 'erself in case Dorrance comes callin' for 'er. But I 'ad people what know people she knew. We got along all right after that."

"Why is she hiding from Dorrance?"

"She thinks Dorrance killed 'er friend."

"I don't believe Dorrance killed her," Paul said. "That's something Creighdor would have one of his men do."

"All she knows is 'er friend wouldn't 'ang 'erself either. So I questioned 'er careful-like. She don't know nuffink about Creighdor. Never seen nobody there what wasn't a patient. Most times there was no one there at all. An' I didn't mention Creighdor's name neither."

"Where is Dorrance?" Matt asked.

"This bird I talked to, she told me Dr. Dorrance got packages from Smithswheel from time to time. Addresses was on the boxes. Always come with two or more men attached to 'em, an' they stayed on with the physician till whatever 'e needed to do was done. Time 'e was finished, the men an' them packages would board the train again. A couple days later, Dorrance would 'ave tickets to Smithswheel brought to 'is 'ouse by a delivery boy."

"That's where he is, then?" Matt asked.

Gabriel shrugged and hooked a thumb over his shoulder at the corpse. "I knew where Edwin Locke was for certain. 'Ad a parish priest what buries the poor 'elp me with that one. But as far as Dorrance bein' in Smithswheel at this moment, I don't know. It's my best guess. He ain't in London that I can find. Course, maybe Creighdor done for 'im an' stuffed 'im in a shallow grave somewheres."

"Matt," Emma said, "even if Dr. Dorrance isn't there, perhaps it might be a good idea to investigate."

Knowing they had nothing else to go on, Matt agreed with a nod. "All right, then."

Except for the electric lights burning in the old textile mill, Smithswheel appeared deserted.

Forty or more houses dotted the valley walls on either side of the small stream that had drawn the community together. Rotting docks for small fishing boats and trade boats occupied the stream banks above and below the forty-foot waterfall centerpiece of the town. In times past, the townsmen had fished the waters and sometimes found their way down to London market to exchange homemade goods for tools and seed crop. Abandoned gardens looked like scabs under the fickle moonlight. Here and there scarecrows stood watch.

Smithswheel was broken into two parts. The bigger, older, and more affluent-looking houses sat on top of the forty-foot drop where the waterfall started. Smaller, more modest houses dotted the land on either side at the bottom of the fall. But rich or poor, the homes had been abandoned years ago.

Smith's Textiles, the company that had given the town its name, sat at the bottom. The large textile building was hunkered up against the hillside. Three stories tall and broader still, the building created an imposing bulk in the dark. The overshot wooden waterwheel nearly matched the forty-foot drop in size. A wooden flume led to the waterbox over the waterwheel, directing a portion of the stream over the buckets that filled and turned the wheel.

The noise from the wheel filled the surrounding area with an uneven thumping echoed by the brightening and dimming of the lights inside the mill. Two gargoyles sat perched atop the roof of the main building. A half-dozen men stood outside the building.

"The gargoyles," Paul whispered, pointing.

Matt nodded. The group hunkered in the shadows of the forest a hundred yards from the mill. It was almost three o'clock in the morning. They had left London as quickly as they had been able, then made the trip to Smithswheel in just under two hours on horseback.

"Means that Creighdor's still about," Gabriel whispered.

"No," Matt said, "but it does mean that something Creighdor values remains here yet."

A grinding, huffing noise sounded off in the distance.

"Train," Jessie said. She held a new 1873-model Winchester lever-action rifle in both hands across her thighs. While getting the horses from the corral her father had rented for his stay in London, she had retreated long enough to get the rifle.

It was the first time Matt had seen the weapon, though he'd heard numerous stories about it. The Winchester was chambered in the same .44-caliber rounds as her pistols, meaning she didn't have to carry different kinds of ammunition as Matt and the others did.

Matt moved through the brush, careful to stay out of sight of the gargoyles perched atop the mill. He didn't know how well the creatures could see in the darkness, but he was willing to wager that their night vision was better than his. He carried a Lee-Metford Mark I rifle, the latest gun adopted by the British infantry, as well as the Webleys. The Lee-Metford held only eight cartridges, but it fired rapidly and smoothly. Jaijo and Narada Chaudhary were similarly equipped.

Paul carried a Whitworth .45-caliber sniper rifle that was capable of accuracy at fifteen hundred yards. The weapon was a favorite of Paul's, an extravagance his father had given him when Roger Hunter offered to teach Paul to shoot as he had Matt.

Gazing to the west, Matt saw the train chugging steadily up-country. An engine, coal car, and two boxcars labored up the grade.

"What's a train doin' 'ere?" Gabriel asked.

"The train line was marked on the map," Matt said.

"Well, if it was, you can bet it ain't been used in years. That's why that lugger's goin' so slow."

"Evidently it's bein' used now," Jessie said. "Want to guess who's usin' it?"

"Creighdor owns a part interest in some train lines," Paul said. "You can wager that he owns that pulling engine and those cars."

"Lookit them sparks comin' off the rails," Gabriel said. "They're lucky they don't set the countryside on fire, they are."

Matt had already noted the way sparks showered from the engine's wheels as the train powered ahead.

"It's from rust build-up on the rails," Emma said. "The iron oxidizes and creates the possibility of sparks. I should think some of those rails would be too worn to be of much use."

"I would hazard a guess," Paul said, "that Creighdor had a team out here replacing the worn sections of track before their use tonight."

"Yes," Narada said. "If you look at the mill as it faces us, you can just catch the gleam of metal there now and again. It is track. And inside the mill, you can see a handcar."

The train continued chugging across the countryside. The exhaust smoke looked gray against the inky blackness of the sky. The noise from the wheels over the tracks blotted out all other sounds.

"What do you think Creighdor's plans are for this place?" Narada asked.

"I'm not sure," Matt said, "but we have to find out." He looked at the group. "Paul, you'll take out the gargoyles when the time comes, if you're able, and cover our retreat. Jaijo, you will stay with him."

Jaijo nodded, his face solemn and set. He still felt strongly that he and his father had no business aiding Matt against Creighdor. He was a reluctant partner at best, but his father's son more than anything.

Without another word Matt led the rest of them forward toward the forbidding mill. He moved low and stayed with the brushline. With the train creating a crescendo of noise, he didn't worry about any sounds they might make. He carried the Lee-Metford rifle forward in both hands.

Only minutes later he came to a halt thirty yards from the mill. He hunkered down as the train clanked to a stop at the end of the railroad spur.

More men got off the train and went inside the mill. Matt counted eight, which meant there were at least fourteen on the premises—*plus the two gargoyles*, he reminded himself—but he had no way of knowing how many were inside.

Atop the building the gargoyles silently kept watch, looking in all directions.

Matt wondered if they thought, if they could take the initiative. Or if they were merely automatons and could not do the first thing without being ordered. Would they know him if they saw him?

The lower floor of the mill glowed with electric light.

Thankfully, whatever refitting Creighdor had ordered done to the interior of the building hadn't included clearing the land outside the mill. Small trees, brush, and tall weeds filled the area. The train had left a swath of broken trees and brush that had grown up through the tracks.

Matt made his way carefully to the engine, remaining out of sight of the gargoyles. Once he was in place and had the Lee-Metford at the ready, he called softly to the others. Gabriel came first, followed by Emma and Jessie, then Narada.

At the front of the engine, two men came out of the building. Matt dodged back and held out a hand to warn the others. They flattened back against the train.

The men talked for a moment, lit pipes for a brief smoke, then took hand trucks from the box-car and headed inside. The combined noise of the locomotive rumbling and the waterwheel grinding kept their words from Matt.

"Round the back," Gabriel whispered into Matt's ear. "Maybe this is the main door, but they're sure to 'ave another back that way. Them who ran this place, why they'd be busy with shipments an' all. They'd want their own entrance."

Matt took the lead again. They all raced down the side of the mill and round the corner. A door was recessed into the wall and sealed with a large lock. He peered through one of the grimy windows.

"An office," Matt told Gabriel. "We can go in here."

"Keep a sharp eye out," Gabriel said, taking out his lock picks.

Narada watched at the corner of the building, crouched so that he remained in the shadows.

A moment later Gabriel turned the doorknob and pushed the door inward. He pointed the shotgun he carried into the room beyond.

Chapter 20

Matt stepped past the others and entered the outer office. Inside the building, the noise from the train and the waterwheel were amplified. The drive shaft squealed as it turned through the center of the three floors of the mill.

A door on the other side of the room let out into the main area. Light seeped into the darkened office from under it.

Easing the door open, Matt looked out and saw armed men carefully carrying small crates down the wide stairs from the main rooms on the second floor. Other men stood guard, all of them armed.

"Bad idea," Gabriel said. "We'd never make it past 'em."

Matt silently agreed. But it wasn't in him to just walk away before he could figure out what Creighdor was doing.

"I've another way," Gabriel said.

Gently Matt closed the door. "What?"

Gabriel pointed at the rear of the room. "Dumbwaiter." He grabbed the narrow wooden chair behind the cobweb-covered desk and jammed it under the door to the outer rooms. "In case we're surprised."

At the back of the room, Gabriel slid open a panel to reveal a dumbwaiter. Matt peered up into the shaft through the slit afforded between the wall and the wooden cage that sat at the end of a rope.

"Prolly used it for sortin' samples an' the like," Gabriel said. "This one's much bigger than the one you'd find in an 'ouse." He pushed at the floor of the cage. "Seems solid enough, all right. If the rope 'asn't given up the ghost, might be enough to get you upstairs."

"Upstairs to what?" Emma demanded. "For all you know, that dumbwaiter may open up into the very room where Creighdor is."

"That's so," Gabriel said. "Truly, it is. But I don't see no other way of gettin' up there to take a look. Them blokes what's carryin' them crates, why they's in a 'urry an' don't look like they'd be any too favorable to questions we might ask anyway."

"We don't have a lot of time," Jessie said. "If they've never brought a train out here before, an' we know that from the way those tracks were all overgrown, then I'm bettin' Creighdor's decided to hoof it outta here quick as he can." She shook her head. "It's now or never. So you just scoot on over because I'm goin' up there for a look-see."

"I will," Matt said, folding himself into the dumbwaiter.

"Narada," Gabriel called as he took hold of the rope. "I'll need some assistance."

Narada put his rifle down and helped pull on the rope.

Slowly the cage jerked and Matt rose up into the shaft. The rifle barely fit into the cage with him. The pulley system overhead squeaked and shrilled so loudly that he was certain he'd be heard. Then he realized that the noises were trapped in the shaft with him. The thumping of the waterwheel and drive as well as the huffing and the puffing of the engine were far more noisy.

He marked the passage of the second story through the cracks between the ill-fitting dumbwaiter door. It was another small area, possibly a supply room. Moonlight peeked through the dirty windows and illuminated the nearly empty shelves.

The dumbwaiter continued up to the third floor. Matt reached for the door at the same time the cage came to a stop and swayed from side to side in the shaft. The door refused to come up at first, then slid out of the way.

Matt saw at once that he was in another office, this one slightly larger than the first. He uncoiled from the dumbwaiter and stepped out, rifle in hand. He heard his own footsteps now and realized that the mill was quieter up on the third story.

The dumbwaiter squeaking behind him almost pushed him into a frenzy. By the time he turned to address Gabriel and let him know to keep the cage still, Emma was emerging from within.

"You shouldn't be here," Matt whispered.

"And you shouldn't be alone," Emma replied. "You're lucky I took the cage before Jessie did. I can only guess what mischief she would get into up here."

"Go back downstairs and wait."

Emma looked at him. "No." Then she walked past him toward the door leading to the main area of the third floor. While Matt was still trying to get himself in order, she opened the door and peeked outside.

"Emma," Matt called.

She turned and gazed back at him, her face wan in the pale moonlight. "No one's there. You should have known that because no light was coming from beneath the door."

Only when she said that did Matt realize that she was right. In the next instant she'd opened the door and gone through.

Cursing to himself, Matt followed. His hands were tight on the rifle.

"I hear voices," Emma said when he joined her.

Through the intermittent slivers of moonlight that slipped inside the mill through cracks in the roof, Matt studied the big room. Weaving looms powered by the driveshaft turned by the waterwheel had once sat in the room. Evidently they had been taken out some time ago, perhaps when the mill had been gutted after business went to the city. Outlines of where the looms had sat still scored the floor.

Bright light stabbed through the gaps in the floor where the boards had rotted away.

Men's voices came from below. Matt instantly recognized one of them as Creighdor's.

Emma cocked her head and tracked the voices. She stopped near the center of the room and knelt down, peering through the cracks between the floorboards. Matt hesitated, hating to get down in a relatively defenseless position. He also knew the others would be anxiously waiting on them to report.

Looking up at him, her ear pressed to the floor, Emma said, "It must be Creighdor." She turned her head, staring down through the crack. "I can see him. And there are the brain parasites." Her voice tightened. "There are *hundreds* of them, Matt!"

Drawn by curiosity as well as the need to know what he was facing, Matt stretched out on the floor. He peered through the crack and listened intently. Several large metal tubs sat against the walls. All of them had water tubes and some kind of metallic poles leading up from them that were connected to electrical wires from the generator. Matt could see brain parasites floating within. Nearby were dozens of glass containers that held five or ten gallons of water each. Men seized the parasites from the tubs and put them into the jars. Matt guessed that the big tanks were in the process of being emptied while the brain parasites were readied for transport.

Creighdor talked to another man in the large room below. At first Matt couldn't identify who it was, then recognized him as Dr. James Dorrance.

"—don't see why we have to leave in the dead of night," Dorrance protested. He paced irritably, stopping at times to peer into glass-walled containers.

"Because you were found out," Creighdor said.

"And that's another thing I don't understand. You keep saying 'they.' 'They found out.' But you've never once mentioned who 'they' are."

"*They*," Creighdor said, "are—at present—my mortal enemies."

"That doesn't make sense," Dorrance said. "The people I saw in my home that night were young. Incredibly young—younger even than you. The two that I got a good look at, the young man and young woman, couldn't have been twenty years old."

"Age has little to do with whether or not an

opponent is dangerous." Creighdor paced the room. He wore evening attire and even carried a top hat. He paused, staring into the large glass containers.

"Age and experience can make an opponent more wily," Creighdor went on, "but baby snakes, for instance, are gifted with a much stronger poison than their adult counterparts." He stroked the glass, drawing a group of the miniature brain parasites after his fingers. "So you see, Dr. Dorrance, their age doesn't matter."

"How did they find out about me?"

"I don't know," Creighdor admitted. "I'm still working on acquiring that knowledge. I thought perhaps your maid might have told them."

"My cleaning lady didn't know those people."

"No. It seems she did not."

Matt thought about how Gabriel had said the cleaning lady had been hanged.

"But she did seem the most likely candidate for talking about the work you're doing for me," Creighdor said. "And, doctor, you have been careless." Creighdor approached a desk covered with papers and a journal. "You let Nigel Kirkland see what you put into his head."

"That was a mistake," Dorrance admitted. "I had not known at the time that he was an opium user. The drugs I administered to him should have kept him sedated long enough for me to complete the insertion."

"Instead, he panicked."

"Yes."

"I was also told that he informed my enemies that you had put something inside his head."

"I didn't know about that."

"No. You don't have policemen hired to watch over you as I do." Creighdor sounded annoyed. "I learned from Mr. Scanlon only minutes ago that Edwin Locke's grave had been robbed."

"Mr. Locke? The moneylender?"

"The very same. Interestingly enough, Mr. Locke's body showed up just before Mr. Scanlon had the good fortune of securing the train outside." Creighdor picked up a human skull from the desk and held it in his hand. "It appears that someone opened Mr. Locke's head. They were looking for something, and I'm quite sure they knew what they were looking for."

"Even so," Dorrance said, "I don't know why I have to give up the laboratory here. The experiments I'm conducting here are too important to be interrupted."

"They're too important to lose." Creighdor placed the skull back on the desk. "Also, I fear you haven't been the model of discretion I require."

Fear showed on Dorrance's face. "What do you mean? I've told no one about you or those creatures or the place."

Creighdor looked at the physician. "Part of the fault is mine and I'll acknowledge it. I have been busy with other endeavors. And other problems. I'm talking about the journals you use to keep records of your experiments here on my behalf. One of them, it appears, is missing."

Dorrance walked to the desk, took out a key, and opened the drawers. "They were all here. Look. See for yourself."

"I have looked." Creighdor reached into the drawer and took a journal out. "This one is blank."

Anxiety tightened Dorrance's face. "They're just mixed up, that's all."

Matt saw the electricity jump through the air then. Thick cables ran from the generator driven by the waterwheel's driveshaft. The cables were connected to small bars sticking out of the fluid-filled containers that held the creatures.

Four men entered the room with hand trucks and loaded up more of the glass containers. Once they had them locked safely into place, they departed.

"You're fortunate that I don't kill you," Creighdor said. "I've killed other men for lesser betrayals."

"Mr. Creighdor, I'm very important to your project," Dorrance said. "Very important. Without me, you wouldn't have been able to alter those creatures so they could survive within a human host. Without me, you wouldn't have been able to breed as many of them as you have." He fidgeted but tried to stand his ground. "I daresay that if I had not accepted your generous offer, you would not have achieved as much in this arena as you had hoped."

"You still have not worked out the creature's weaknesses," Creighdor said.

"I will. I give you my word on that. No one else can do that for you. Even if you brought someone new into this assignment, it would delay your work by months if not a year or more."

Creighdor chuckled, but the sound didn't hold much mirth. "I find you useful yet, Dr. Dorrance. Never fear. But you will not be given the same kind of freedom you've had in the past."

"Thank you, sir."

"And if you betray me in the future," Creighdor promised in a cold voice, "I'll kill you where you stand."

Dorrance shivered. "Yes, sir."

"See to it the rest of these containers are properly loaded," Creighdor ordered.

Dorrance said that he would.

Creighdor left without another word.

"All right," Matt whispered. "We've got to act. They're already splitting those creatures up."

Emma hesitated. "There is so much we could learn."

Matt studied her. The bright light splintering through the gapped floorboards illuminated her features. "Emma, those creatures are evil."

"They're different. We know hardly anything about them. We don't even know where they're from. Possibly South America. That's what I would guess if I had to. So many strange things—animal, insect, and plant—live there in those tropical jungles. Paul said that Creighdor did business there. Perhaps one of his associates found these things there and he learned how to use them."

"He's got hundreds of those things," Matt said carefully. "Think about it. If Creighdor were able to infect hundreds of people in London— royalty, captains of industry, the Queen's court— do you realize how much power he would wield?"

"I know, but—"

"No." Matt stood. "We'll slip out of here. Once they have the train loaded, all of these things will be in one spot. We can ambush the train, blow it up. If we get lucky, perhaps we can end the threat of the creatures as well as that of Creighdor." He felt the weight of the dynamite sticks in the satchel across his back. Gabriel hadn't stinted on the munitions supply and they'd come ready to wage a war if they had to.

"Guards!" Dorrance yelled from below.

Thinking the worst, Matt hunkered down again. Before they tried going back through the dumbwaiter, as slow and as vulnerable as that was, he needed to know what had happened.

Perhaps one of his friends had been discovered.

Looking down, Matt saw Dorrance pointing up at the ceiling. Too late Matt realized that his and Emma's shifting on the floor had sent a thin stream of dust and dirt between the cracks and into the water containers below filled with brain parasites.

Three of Creighdor's men ran into the room and unlimbered their weapons.

"The ceiling!" Dorrance yelled. "Someone is there!"

"Time to go!" Matt pushed himself to his feet and reached for Emma's hand. If they hurried, they might be able to make the two-story drop to the ground outside through the window. There was a good chance the fall wouldn't injure them too badly to run.

Bullets hammered the ceiling where Emma had been. The rounds tore through, leaving big holes and splintered wood that was already rotten with age and neglect. Before Emma could run, the rotten wood beneath her fragmented.

She fell.

Matt felt her fingers slip right through his hand. "Emma!" His sudden fear ripped her name from his lips.

Gripping the rifle, he peered down through the hole and took aim at one of the men. He hated the thought that he was about to take a man's life.

It's war, he told himself. *They're the enemy.*

More than that, they were already advancing on Emma, who was struggling to get up from the floor.

Chapter 21

When Matt pulled the trigger, the rifle slammed back against his shoulder. He watched as the first man crumpled. The other two men fired at him blindly, trying to get away. He shot one of the two survivors, but one of them escaped, fleeing down the stairs and bawling out the alarm.

Matt dropped through the hole in the floor and landed beside Emma. A quick survey assured him that she was all right and had only had the breath knocked out of her. He helped her to her feet, then shoved them both behind the desk as one of Creighdor's men appeared at the stairwell and started firing.

Thankfully, the desk proved resilient enough to withstand the bullets.

"We're in a tight spot," Matt shouted to Emma above the noise of the gunfire and the waterwheel. He fed rounds into the rifle to replace the ones he'd fired, then slung the weapon and reached into his pockets for the dynamite.

Taking a lucifer from his pocket and striking it with his thumbnail, he lit the fuses of two dynamite bundles and threw them under the glass containers of brain parasites on either side of the big room. Using the knife from his boot, he cut half the fuse off a third stick of dynamite. Striking another lucifer, he lit the third stick and threw it toward the stairwell.

"Down," Matt commanded, covering Emma's body with his own.

The third dynamite stick blew up only seconds later, turning a big section of the stairwell into kindling and igniting several fires. The other two dynamite sticks had longer fuses.

"Up," Matt ordered, drawing both Webley pistols from his coat pockets and hooking a wrist under Emma's arm to get her to her feet.

Emma swung into motion at once, grabbing Dorrance's journals from the desk.

Matt started to tell her that they didn't have time, that the dynamite might go off and bring the whole mill down on top of them. Then he caught a flicker of movement coming up on his right. He started to turn, then received a blow to the head that dropped him to his knees and sent his senses spinning. He tasted blood inside his mouth.

Dr. Dorrance whipped a piece of a fallen ceiling board at Emma. Matt tried to shout a warning but couldn't. Placing the barrel of a Webley against the floor, he tried to lever himself up so he could bring the other pistol to bear.

Emma lithely dodged the physician's attack. Before Dorrance could recover, she swung the thick stack of journals and knocked him backward. The doctor flailed and slid on the debris on the floor. In two quick steps, he fell backward into one of the big tubs of brain parasites.

Dorrance never had a chance. Though he struggled to come out of the water, the brain parasites made for him at once, moving inhumanly fast.

If you're in the water with them, Matt realized, *you'd never be able to avoid them.*

The creatures invaded Dorrance's ears, his eyes, nose, and his screaming mouth. Dozens of them poured in. He shuddered and quivered. His hands hooked the sides of the metal tub and he tried to pull himself out. But his strength left him and he dropped back into the tub. In the next heartbeat, the water began to turn crimson.

Emma stood frozen, her hand covering her mouth in horror. She'd sliced open corpses without hesitation, but the sight of sudden death overwhelmed her.

Senses still reeling, Matt hooked his arm through her elbow and pulled her into motion again. They ran. He had no idea how much time they had before the dynamite went off, but it couldn't be much.

He didn't even pause at the storeroom door that was in line with the dumbwaiter, shoving it forward and entering the room just behind Emma. Pulling open the dumbwaiter door, Matt yelled down to Gabriel, "We're coming down!"

"Come on with you then," Gabriel called back up. "Things is gettin' mighty lively round 'ere right now."

Holding the books close to her with one arm, Emma used the other to lever herself down into the dumbwaiter shaft. She let go and dropped. Narada helped her recover. Matt was at her heels.

"Move!" Matt ordered.

Gabriel led the way, pausing at the door to make certain the way was clear, then running through. The others raced after him. Matt was at the door when the first of the explosives detonated.

With the dynamite bundles against the opposite sides of the room, the blasts tore out a large section of the support beams. Concussive force hurled Matt through the door. He picked himself up and ran, glancing over his shoulder as the mill came apart.

The structure sagged in the middle first, then teetered and fell toward the train. Several men who had escaped the blast inside had raced outside and were now trying to raise their weapons to use against Matt and the others. Instead, the mill tumbled down on them, burying them under tons of debris.

"Look out!" Narada shouted, lifting the rifle he carried.

For the first time, Matt realized he'd left his own rifle inside the mill. He took out his pistols and followed Narada's line of sight.

A gargoyle spread its wings suddenly and blotted out the moon as it streaked for Emma. Matt brought his pistols to bear but missed four times. Narada's rounds tore holes in its chest and left leg.

Just as the gargoyle was about to reach Emma, its head came apart and it dropped like a rock.

Nice shot, Paul, Matt thought, knowing it had to have been Paul's sharpshooting skills with the Whitworth that had saved the day. He searched for the second gargoyle, wondering if Paul had already disposed of it or if the creature had gone down with the building.

Then the mound of debris that had swept over the train started shifting. Gray smoke billowed out from the stack. In the next instant the pulling engine's wheels grabbed hold of the track, yanking the coal car and boxcar free.

Matt started forward at once.

As soon as the train cleared the debris, three men hung out the sides of the open boxcar and started shooting. One of the bullets caught Narada and knocked him to the ground.

Matt dived for cover and crawled over to

Narada. The man had been hit in the thigh and there was a lot of blood.

Please, Matt thought, *don't let the bullet have hit an artery. He'll bleed out before we can do anything. I don't want to have to tell his wife that he lost his life because of me.*

Jessie's pistols barked rapidly. In the distance past Narada, Matt saw one of the gunmen tumble from the train as it gained speed down the tracks.

Matt pressed his hands against Narada's wound to stop the blood.

Narada's face was knotted up in pain. He was pale, going into shock. "Creighdor has those creatures aboard the train. Whatever he was planning to do with them, he still can."

"I know." Matt put more pressure on the wound. He cursed. *Isn't it going to stop bleeding?* His hands were already drenched in crimson. *It's got to stop bleeding!* He remembered how he had seen his father die. Narada was slowly fading.

"You've got to go after him," Narada said.

"We can't catch that train." Matt stared at it, seeing it picking up speed now on the downgrade.

"The horses," Jessie said. "We can catch it with the horses."

"They're a quarter mile from here," Matt said. As he watched, Paul's marksmanship took another of the gunmen from the boxcar.

"The track curves around back behind the

horses," Jessie said. "If we hurry, we might be able to cut it off." Without another word she was up and gone, running cross-country.

"Jessie!" Matt called.

She kept running.

"Go after her," Narada said. "She can't do it by herself."

"I can't leave you." Matt felt torn. It was one thing to lead the others while they were a group, but trying to figure out what to do now was impossible.

"You have to." Narada fisted Matt's shirt, but his hand shook. "That man killed my brother. He killed your father. He cannot be allowed to escape. There is no telling what he will be able to do with those unholy creatures."

Matt looked for Jessie and saw that she was already a hundred yards away.

"Go," Narada urged, pushing at Matt.

"I've got him," Emma said. "I can take care of him."

Matt looked at her. "Don't," he said, intending to tell her, *Don't let him die*, but finding the words wouldn't come around the stone of pain in his throat.

"I won't," Emma said. "I swear to you that I won't." She slid his hands away and put her hands over Narada's leg. "Gabriel, tear off the bottom of your shirt. I need to make a pressure bandage."

"Gabriel," Matt said, shrugging out of his coat

to lose the extra weight and picking up his pistols, "stay with them."

"I will. You be careful. Jessie, she won't back off from nuffink. An' I think she'll catch that bloody train. Don't let 'er do it alone."

Matt stood and ran. He focused on Jessie, seeing her impossibly far ahead of him. Thoughts of his father came to him. Memories of his mother, of the times they'd spent in her greenhouse, spun through his mind. He thought about Nigel Kirkland, sitting in jail with the brain parasite nibbling away at him, growing bigger and bigger.

Whom had Creighdor infected with the horrors so far? How many others could he infect with the deadly cargo aboard the train?

The Webleys felt like anvils at the ends of Matt's arms. He knew he could have gone faster without them, but he would have been left almost defenseless. He kept them in a tight grip and ran faster.

Paul said something as Matt sped by him, but Matt wasn't paying attention. He didn't have the breath left. Everything in his body screamed out for more air. He made himself keep breathing and not quit.

He gained on Jessie. Despite the fact that they were nearly of a height, he was moving quicker, with longer strides. Then he saw that she still carried the Winchester.

The train faded out of sight over a hill, gray smoke puffing against the night.

Less than two hundred yards from where they'd left the horses in a shallow wrinkle in the valley, Matt caught up with her.

Jessie glanced over her shoulder and surprise colored her face. Giving him a somber nod, she somehow picked up her pace, matching his stride.

They were neck and neck when they reached the horses, both too winded to speak.

Matt shook the reins free from a branch and pulled himself up on his horse, swinging into the saddle.

Jessie ran up behind hers, placed both hands on the horse's rump, and vaulted into the saddle as if the feat were nothing. She leaned forward to pull the reins free, then put her heels to her horse's flanks and was the first one out of the gate.

As he wheeled his mount around, Matt saw Paul struggling to catch up, still a hundred yards out. He let the horse have its head, following Jessie through the forest, trusting her sense of direction.

They rode through trees and up and down hills. The moon showed them no favor. Matt clipped the Webleys by their butt rings to shoulder straps and the pistols beat at him. A brief check in the saddlebags showed him that he had more dynamite there. Gabriel had been awfully successful.

The horse's speed surprised Matt. Both of them

were breeds he wasn't familiar with, smaller and more sure-footed. Jessie had called them mustangs and said they were a true product of the American West.

Matt heard the train before he saw it come over the last rise. It was moving under a full head of steam, throwing sparks from the wheels and the tracks.

A man clinging to the boxcar lifted his pistol and fired.

Matt heard a bullet cut the wind right beside his ear.

Jessie stood in her stirrups and brought the Winchester to her shoulder while at a full gallop. She fired, levered the action, and fired again.

One or both bullets caught the man and he pitched from the boxcar.

Gripping the saddlebags, Matt guided his mount close to the boxcar. He glanced at Jessie. She slung her rifle and reached down for his reins. When they were close enough, Matt drew his feet up to the saddle, then launched himself over into the boxcar.

He hit and rolled, sliding out of control for one wild instant and nearly going through the open door on the other side of the car. He maintained his hold on the saddlebags.

Standing, he looked at the containers of liquid that held the brain parasites. Straw cushioned the floor and the packing crates filled with sealed jars.

He thought he could feel the malevolence of the creatures inside. Even as he prepared the dynamite, he couldn't help wondering where Creighdor had gotten the creatures, how he'd brought gargoyles to life, and how Josiah Scanlon could withstand being shot in the chest at point-blank range. There was so much he didn't know about the man.

Jessie's Winchester barked sharply three times.

Glancing up as he struck a lucifer, Matt saw Lucius Creighdor clinging to the side of the box-car. Before Matt could move, Creighdor swung around the boxcar door and kicked him in the face.

Matt dropped the match and dynamite and flew backward. He reached for the Webleys, discovering that one had torn free somewhere along the way and that the other was caught by the crates. By the time he'd freed the pistol, Creighdor was on him.

Creighdor hit Matt so hard his head whipped to one side and he almost lost consciousness. Cursing, the older man reached for him.

"I would have let you live, Matthew Hunter," Creighdor said. "All you had to do was stay out of my business." He reached behind him and closed the boxcar door, shutting out Jessie even as she fired.

The rifle bullet tore through the wooden door.

Matt struggled to free the Webley. In the same

moment, he saw that the dropped match had caught the dry straw on fire. Smoke floated, then the train hit a rough spot on the track and scattered the pool of flames in a half-dozen directions, catching more straw on fire.

And Creighdor was so intent on Matt he hadn't yet noticed.

"There are things I believe you know," Creighdor said. In an amazing feat of strength, he bent one of the iron bars framing the boxcar door and jammed it. "Things I think your father told you that I would like to know."

Matt yanked on the Webley, feeling the pistol loosen in the grip of whatever was holding it.

"With your father dead," Creighdor went on, "I was certain I could get his secrets from you. I think he outsmarted himself, though. I think he managed to keep them from you as well."

Matthew, the only way two men can keep a secret is if one of them is dead.

Matt heard his father's voice distinctly. And in that moment came clarity. He felt the weight of the iron key against his chest. The hiding place was almost impossible, but it was the only place to look. And it made perfect sense.

"So that makes you just another irritation to be swatted away," Creighdor said over the rumble of the wheels rolling across the tracks. He stepped forward.

Feeling the Webley come free, Matt pointed it and pulled the trigger. Creighdor was less than ten feet away. Even with the jarring motion of the boxcar, Matt didn't think he could miss.

All six rounds caught Creighdor in the chest, driving him backward. Bright green spots on his shirtfront marked the places where he'd been hit.

Matt fully expected the man to fall down dead.

Instead, Creighdor threw back his head and roared with laughter. "There's so much you'll never know."

Throttling the primitive fear that filled him, Matt said, "There's one thing I know."

Creighdor looked amused.

"Your cargo is on fire."

Bewildered, perhaps only then smelling the smoke, Creighdor turned. By that time, the whole other end of the boxcar was ablaze. Flames ran up the end wall and touched its ceiling. And the bundle of dynamite was lost somewhere in the straw.

Cursing, Creighdor bent to pick up one of the bottles of brain parasites.

Pushing up from the floor, Matt hurled himself at Creighdor. He managed to knock him through the remaining open boxcar door. Incredibly, Creighdor caught hold of the doorframe. The landscape beside the track went by with dizzying pace as the train sped along.

Creighdor hit Matt in the face, knocking him back inside. Before he could get to his feet again, Creighdor slammed the door shut from the outside.

"You may have cost me this cargo," Creighdor roared through the closed door, "but I'll take your life."

Feeling the heat of the blaze, Matt pushed himself up and staggered to the door. He pulled but couldn't open it. Creighdor had locked or jammed it from outside.

"Die, Matthew Hunter," Creighdor shouted. "I hope you're in agony for a good long time while that boxcar burns down around you."

With both doors now closed, the car quickly filled with smoke from the burning straw. Struggling to breathe, Matt thought quickly. Peering at the other end of the boxcar, he saw that the fire had already burned through. The hole offered a way out, but he couldn't get to it.

Then he remembered the brain parasites. He picked up one of the nearby bottles and threw it at the stacks on the far end of the compartment. Several of the bottles shattered and fluid rained out over the burning straw, briefly extinguishing the flames.

Choking and coughing, head spinning and aware of the danger of both the lost dynamite and the freed brain parasites, Matt threw two more bottles into the corner to extinguish more fire, then ran through the flaming straw down the middle. He climbed the wrecked, half-burned crates and scrambled to the top of the boxcar wall. Glass cut his fingers and embers burned his flesh, but he vaulted up to the top of the boxcar.

Rolling over to the middle of the roof, he sucked in the clean air. At the same time, he felt the heat of the fire trapped inside. Despite the wet area he'd created, he knew the boxcar was swiftly turning into an inferno.

And the dynamite was somewhere inside.

"Matt!"

Still coughing, Matt barely heard Jessie's voice over the rumble of the train. He looked down and saw her galloping alongside the train, still holding the reins to his horse.

"Jump!" Jessie called up.

Matt didn't want to jump, but he knew that Jessie wouldn't quit trying to save him. And if she stayed alongside the train when the dynamite went off, she would be killed or badly injured.

Picking his time, Matt slid over to the edge of the boxcar and dropped, landing on top of his mount. The horse stumbled for a moment, and Matt felt certain they were going to fall. He'd just managed to get the horse straightened away when the dynamite blew up.

The boxcar exploded into a million flaming pieces, leaving only the warped iron frame of the undercarriage intact.

Amazingly, the rest of the train wasn't destroyed in the explosion. It sped down the tracks.

Jessie pulled their horses up. "We can't catch them," she said.

Matt nodded, still trying to get his lungs full of clean air to take the place of the smoke he'd inhaled.

"Nothing inside that car survived," Jessie said. "Was Creighdor in there? I saw him for a time."

"No," Matt answered. "Creighdor wasn't in there." And he didn't know if the explosion would have killed him anyway.

Epilogue

One day later, his bandaged hands still tender from the superficial burns he'd suffered during the boxcar escape, Matt entered the cemetery at the family estate. He'd buried his father there in the rain only three weeks ago, and the memory still haunted him.

"You could be wrong, you know," Paul said.

For a moment, Matt stood outside the vault where Roger Hunter had been laid. He took the iron key from the leather strap around his neck.

"I'm not," Matt said. "'The only way two men can keep a secret is if one of them is dead.' He told me that from time to time. I thought it was morbid, but he always found humor in it."

"And if you don't find a keyhole in there that will fit that key? Will you be able to bear the disappointment?"

"It will be there." Matt entered the vault and walked down the row of dead ancestors to his father's crypt. He knelt and went over the mortised limestone wall behind his father's crypt.

It took ten minutes, and Matt could tell that Paul was on the verge of giving up. They'd had a hard time of it. Narada was still bedridden with the wound to his thigh, and Jessie was overwrought about the parasite living inside her father's head. Emma was certain she would find a cure for the creatures in Dorrance's notes, but she was working herself to exhaustion translating all the journals from the doctor's coded entries.

Creighdor and Scanlon had seemingly vanished from the face of the earth again, despite Gabriel's best efforts to find them.

The keyhole was at the back of the crypt, cunningly fashioned so it just looked like a chip out of the mortar. If Matt hadn't been convinced it was there, he would never have found it.

Paul stared in rapt fascination as Matt thrust the key in and turned.

A section of the crypt fell out near the bottom. Inside was a cavity that held a thick book.

Matt extracted the book and flipped it open. A letter lay on top.

Dearest Matthew,

If you have had to seek this out, you will know that Creighdor is a vicious and cunning opponent, and that he has unearthly knowledge and weapons.

I knew eventually you would remember what I always said about secrets. You've always been a clever boy. Now the time has come for you to be a clever man.

I have much to tell you, and I will. This book is filled with truth and knowledge that you can use against Creighdor. If you are courageous and resourceful, you can triumph over that base-hearted villain.

The way will not be easy. My death, I am sure, is a grim reminder of that.

The first thing you must do, my boy, which I am endeavoring to do, is find a mummy named Pasebakhaenniut. There is a fascinating legend about him. It seems that his death three thousand years ago might not have been as final as most would believe.

In fact, Pasebakhaenniut's death is only one of the beginnings. . . .

ABOUT THE AUTHOR

Mel Odom is the author of many novels for adults, teens, and middle-grade readers. He lives with his family in Oklahoma. Visit him at www.melodom.net.

THE SECOND MRS. GIOCONDA

E.L. Konigsburg

A page-turning exploration of
the puzzle behind Leonardo da Vinci's
most famous masterpiece

"[Konigsburg] gives an
intriguing look at the life
of Leonardo da Vinci and
helps us understand why
The Mona Lisa became
such a loved masterpiece."
—*Los Angeles Times*

1-4169-0342-9
(Simon Pulse)

0-689-82121-2
(Aladdin Paperbacks)

Simon Pulse ∞ Simon & Schuster ∞ www.SimonSaysTEEN.com

feel the fear.

FEAR STREET® NIGHTS

A brand-new Fear Street trilogy by the master of horror

R.L. STINE

In Stores Now

Simon Pulse
Published by Simon & Schuster